Hidden Family Gems

Hidden Family Gems

THE ARDENDALE MYSTERIES SERIES

FELICITY FOX

Published by Author Academy Elite
PO Box 43, Powell, OH 43065
www.AuthorAcademyElite.com

Identifiers:
Library of Congress Control Number: 2019916990
Paperback: 978-1-64085-984-5
Hardback: 978-1-64085-985-2
Ebook: 978-1-64085-986-9

Available in paperback, hardback, e-book, and audiobook

Some names and identifying details have been changed to protect the privacy of individuals.

A Note from the Author

One morning like any other, my dad called me. I don't think he even said hi but immediately began with a story. I listened along, not really knowing where he was going with it, but found myself extra-interested in the story that day. Then, he said, "I dreamt this. You should write a book about this." (I think my siblings and I get our vivid, crazy dreams from our dad.) I remember thinking about that dream as the days passed. Somehow, I felt as though I *needed* to write the story, so I sat down and began typing. This was out of my comfort zone because I felt better equipped to write children's books, not young adult novels. Then, on a trip across the US to be a bridesmaid in my dear friend's wedding, the storyline emerged from my fingertips! Before I knew it, I wrote this book, and soon thereafter, I had the outline of the sequel jotted down.

It brings joy to my heart to be able to share this story! My dad's parents—my grandparents—were business owners in real life. In fact, they were once named "Business People of the Year" and ran more than one company in their many years here on earth. (You'll notice I fit that true award into the story.) So, while "Pop and Gram" in this story run a different store, and characters and storylines are completely made up, the successful business is not far-fetched. I called my grandparents "Pop and Gram," and my hometown is small and picturesque, like Ardendale. And with great joy, I wrote this story with my mom's family in mind as well. Like Stephenie Meyer did in the *Twilight* series, I used family and friend names and little details that I intricately weaved in to create special moments.

Oh, and regarding Ardendale . . . well, my dad thought up that name. When he gave me a hoodie with the name "Ardendale" imprinted on it that he had ordered, I continued on with this vision.

To my dad—the initial inspiration behind this book. When he called me to tell me about his vivid dream, little did I know it would become the book you're reading. My dad is my protector, my pun joke partner, and a source of immense joy in my life. I love you so much! *Lovey, lovey, lovey.* And to my mom—using the name "Maude" meant so much. *You* mean so much to me. You're my biggest cheerleader, my best friend, and I love you so much! *Lovey, lovey, lovey.*

Chapter One

The multi-colored crocheted afghan laid across the back of the couch. Maude leaned over and inhaled the scent of baby powder and stale pretzels that permeated the cozy, handmade blanket. The couch was an ugly shade of dirty yellow and olive green. Four wooden legs proudly held it up from the generic, hides-the-dirt-well, brown rug. Maude was nineteen years old with long, wavy, reddish-brown hair, a slender figure, and deep green, almond-shaped eyes. In her dark green khaki pants and a white and green horizontally striped sweater, she reached over for her iced tea on the end table. The lemon hanging off the side of the glass dripped slow trickles onto the flower-patterned napkin beneath it. The two-level end table held an old-fashioned plug-in lamp with ancient metal arms. It was amazing that it hadn't caught fire yet. It sat on a plain yellow crocheted doily, and when the lamp got hot, it smelled like burning metal, but without a trace of melting anywhere. Pop always said they don't make things like they used to. She supposed he was right.

The couch was virtually spotless despite the maroon-colored dog bed a few feet to its left. Copper wasn't allowed on the couch, but Maude assumed all pet owners were afflicted with dog hair on their furniture and clothes. She had wanted a dog as a child, but her mom was allergic. Her dad told her that her mom, Hazel, used to purchase store-bought pet fish and enthusiastically tried to dissuade her daughter from wanting a fur animal.

"Maude, Mommy is allergic to dogs and cats, sweetie. We have to stick with fish and beautiful fish tanks," her mom used to say.

Therefore, Maude's experience with dogs only occurred while at friends' houses.

When she glanced over at Copper, the gorgeous female Doberman her grandparents had aptly named her due to her copper-colored coat, she remembered the longing for a fur animal. Of course, she realized Copper was a unique Doberman. Pop trained her to be calm and to love people. In fact, Maude didn't think she ever heard her bark.

Nevertheless, people were intimidated, assuming a big Doberman was vicious.

Pop used to say, "That is the point. Copper will protect us if she needs to, but not unless we tell her to or if she senses she needs to. She is gentle and loving and never runs off or needs a leash. Anyone who intends harm will probably stay away when they see a *vicious* Doberman around."

Maude remembered when Pop told her this he was sitting in his royal blue recliner. Copper's dog tags had chimed as Pop pulled her over for a hug. She remembered her dad saying he felt comforted because an assumed mean, big dog, meant hopefully no one would ever hurt his parents.

Pop and Gram, as Maude called them, were both in their seventies, still healthy, and able to get around well. They owned and operated a local bookstore for nearly fifty years, but the time had come that they needed more managerial help. Their bookstore, The Books Are Here, was open seven days a week and had many faithful employees. The store was in great shape thanks to the help of their most trusted employee, their store manager, Kay. Kay, however, wanted to semi-retire within the next year but still work part-time. It is possible that Maude, her grandparents, and perhaps the town could never know a more genuine, kind, patient, hardworking, and Christian woman than Kay. Maude knew her parents relied on her whole-heartedly to keep things in order in the business. Of course, fortunately the store also always had customer service floor leaders on duty too. But it was the news of Kay's retirement that turned Maude's life upside down. Because her dad was an only child, he and Maude were all her grandparents had. At eighteen, her dad moved away to attend prestigious Columbia University, then Columbia Law School, and immediately landed a job as a lawyer, even making partner within the firm. Although he visited frequently, he never planned to return to the small town where he grew up. He settled into his career, content in his location.

Maude's life, however, was unsettled. She graduated high school, had done one semester of a liberal arts college, but hadn't settled on a concentration. It was difficult to ignore the fact that her favorite part about visiting her grandparents was spending time in their store. As a little girl, she sat in the store front window writing stories with sharpened pencils and a zippered case of erasers. At night, she read books. Each morning, she had pretend-tea like someone from their café would. She used an old messenger bag from the store for her books and notebooks and pencils and erasers and pretended to be a businesswoman. Pop and Gram told her she could have the business someday. But she was young at the time and never really thought that day would come.

When her college semester ended, Maude came to visit for an extended stay. It was officially summertime, and with no other plans, she planned to stay for a few weeks. Before she left home, her dad told her to be open-minded because her grandparents wanted to "discuss her future." She guessed it was about the bookstore but thought it might be helping there, not something huge like *staying* there! Oh, how wrong she was. On her first night there during dinner, they brought it up after Gram served the roast beef. "Honey, thank you for visiting!" she said. "We just love it when you come. While you're here, we would like to talk to you about the future—*your* future."

Nervous, Maude kept her mouth full of food to avoid having to speak. Gram continued, "Honey, we are at the age that we need to consider the future of our business and home. You have bloomed into a beautiful young woman, and you and your dad are the only family we have. William has made a successful career for himself and won't return home. We understand that. But we built the bookstore from nothing fifty years ago and certainly would love to keep it in the family. As the years have gone on, we notice your knack for the atmosphere, and well, we'd like to give you the business." Maude was speechless. Gram grabbed a paper towel and wiped the counter. "We don't want to overwhelm you, honey. We understand you are young. But we are able to teach you everything you'll need to know, and certainly, we'll still be around. We're going to live forever, after all!" They all exchanged smiles.

Maude struggled to find words. She felt extremely honored to be thought of so highly. "Wow," was all she managed to say at first. Then, she continued, "Pop and Gram, what an honor. But this is a lot to absorb." She grabbed her glass and sipped some lemonade. They sat in silence, so she felt compelled to continue. "Clearly, you all know I'm unsettled in college. Not to sound corny, but I haven't found my *path*." Maude gave air quotes with a smile. "The thing is, I know I'm only nineteen, but . . ."

She took a bite of her food as Gram sat down across from her. Leaning forward, Gram placed her veiny hand on hers. Maude smiled at the comforting gesture but didn't really know what to say. Her grandparents didn't seem to want to pressure her and allowed the silence. Soon, Maude continued, "I love to read and write. That has been a consistent thing in my life." She realized she didn't want to commit either way yet. Was she in love with the idea of relocating to Ardendale permanently? Well, she didn't *hate* it. She happened to like the simplicity this place offered, and her grandparents' store was always her most favorite place. "I'm not sure what else to say except thank you, and I am honored," she choked up as she said the words that they would no doubt be delighted to hear.

"Oh, honey! You are our girl! How about we show you a little bit more behind-the-scenes this week, see how you feel, you know, to get your feet wet a little? Does that work for you?" Gram stood up and walked over to Maude's chair, leaned down, and held Maude in an embrace.

Maude agreed but felt herself wishing her mom was alive so she could talk this over with her. Her mom, Hazel, passed from a rare blood disease when Maude was four. She remembered four things about her mom—her hair was the same color reddish-brown as Maude has; she had a tiny bone structure and stood only five feet tall; she smelled like lilacs or maybe Maude thought she did because they were her favorite flower. The last memory was Maude's favorite. She remembered her mom watching *The Carol Burnett Show*.

After dinner that night, Maude went for a walk. The tree-lined street had no lilac trees in sight, but she swore she could smell them. This occasionally happened to her, and she firmly believed that when it did, her mom was with her. Why else would she smell lilacs? Maude didn't want to talk out loud for fear the neighbors would think she was crazy, but she smiled and thought, *What do I do, Mom?* A breeze blew up out of nowhere and tickled behind her right ear. Maude looked to her right, and though she didn't see anything, she knew it had to be her mom. This sort of thing happened often, and it brought her such peace that she knew it was the answer she was looking for. Maude should give this town and the business a chance.

That night, Maude settled in early and fell asleep quickly. She whispered *Thank you* in her heart to her mom for the peace and had a good night's sleep. The next morning it seemed funny to go from visiting a place she loved to actually knowing it was about to be *hers*. But she felt braver than she had the previous evening and proceeded to get ready for the day. Knowing she should wear something other than jeans, she decided on a plain blue spring dress and black leggings and headed to the front door as she swung on her jean jacket. *Ah, these simple white sandals will do the trick,* she thought as she slipped them on. Grabbing her purse, she locked the door behind her and walked the short few blocks to The Books Are Here.

She bought a vanilla chai latte at the AM to PM Café that was inside the store. Maude chuckled at the name of the café. "PM" stood for her grandparents' names, Philly and Marguerite. Because they realized people might not know what "PM" stood for, and they may assume it meant nighttime, Pop and Gram created the unique name. They thought they should add "AM" to mean morning. Maude looked around and smiled at the students doing homework at the tables. She noticed older people reading books, parents socializing, a group of women knitting, and a few people sitting by themselves with their tablets or laptops. Frank Sinatra was playing over the speakers in the ceiling.

She smiled because Frank Sinatra was one of Gram's favorite singer's. Years ago over a dinner conversation during one of her visits with Pop and Gram, they were discussing "Ol' blue eyes,"

Frank Sinatra. His version of "I'll Be Home for Christmas" was playing, and Pop was singing along. It was a few days before Christmas, and Pop was serving spaghetti and meatballs that evening. Why Maude so vividly remembered that night was because that same night they watched *White Christmas*. Maude had never seen it, and that was when Pop said they liked to play Bing Crosby or Sinatra's Christmas albums at the store because they were Gram's favorite musical artists. Maude remembered the night and the conversation as though it had just happened.

Truthfully, that was also the beginning of Maude's love for their music as well. Her friends called her old-fashioned, but the friendly banter didn't offend her. She considered herself a loner because she always seemed to do her own thing. She wasn't athletic, though she did play field hockey for a couple of years to give it a try. She found she preferred the arts and joined the Drama Club and S.A.D.D. instead. She was an avid reader and liked to sing in church. She wasn't one to join a trend, peer pressure didn't affect her, and others' opinions didn't bother her.

With her latte in hand, she headed back to the office. The back of the store had what Maude still thought of as a *secret* section. A pass-coded door just to the left of the customer restrooms led to four rooms. One, an office her grandparents shared with filing cabinets, two desks, laptops, and endless paperwork. Second, a break room with a refrigerator and two tables with many more chairs than space allotted. The break room also had coffee, tea, cold beverages, and snacks. A third room had storage, including tables, chairs, shelves, books, and many other bookstore-related things. The fourth room was a staff restroom. Pop and Gram were in their office and greeted her with smiles and waves.

"Maudie! You look just lovely, dear." Gram smiled.

"You're beautiful," Pop chimed in.

With a folder in her hand, Gram handed over another one. "So, normally I'd give you a tour of the place, show you where the fire extinguisher and emergency lighting system are located, but you've been through that," Gram said with a chuckle. Maude recalled a time when she was younger and a device within AM to PM Café was accidentally left on. The fire department came, but thankfully, there was never a fire, just alarms and some smelly smoke for a few hours. It's interesting how some things stay with you because, since that single event, she was very aware of the emergency areas, devices, and protocols.

"Do you know that was one of the only two times we've ever had the fire department here?" Pop interrupted her thoughts.

"I was unaware of a second time! What? When? Obviously, there must not have been any damage or we would have heard." Maude looked at the ceiling as though she expected to see black marks from a fire.

"Morrie broke the fire alarm and didn't even need an axe to do it!" Pop laughed. He looked off to the upper corner of the room, smiled, and shook his head. "Marguerite, remember when Morrie left the water on in the restroom sink overnight?"

"What a character! Imagine if he was still around? It seemed we had a new story each week about something he forgot, dropped, broke, or ran into. God bless him." Gram touched her hand to her heart.

"Morrie was an older gentleman. After retirement, he wanted something part time and despite the endless stories of his mishaps, he really did try hard, and honestly, we could rely on him to be here when we needed. But boy, he was prone to klutziness. It was amusing. He jammed the step ladder into the fire alarm on accident, so the alarms went off like the fourth of July. Let's see, once he spilled his coffee on a pile of magazines, forgot to put things back—that happened a few times—left the water running. My goodness, he'd leave the walkie-talkie on a shelf, which meant it was dead the next day, which happened a *lot*. Alas, he *was* a good worker, always on time, did his tasks as asked—and for the record, these were amusing little things and easy to accept—but by golly, he was accident-prone," Pop said.

"He's since passed away. What a beautiful soul who left us with warm memories!" Gram smiled and returned a file to the cabinet.

Just then, there was a knock on the door. "Come on," Pop responded.

Maude chuckled. For some reason, Pop always said, 'Come on' instead of 'Come in.' But what she hadn't known is he also says it at work.

"Maude! Dear Maude! How wonderful to see you!" Kay entered the room and embraced Maude. She wore a black floor-length dress with piano keys sprinkled on it, along with a smock. Maude smiled at the unique dress. Kay gave private piano lessons, and Maude realized she could probably offer more availability for more students when she semi-retired. The smock over the dress was the only *uniform* required along with business-casual attire. You could wear a collared shirt, but it didn't need to be a button up. You could wear khakis or cotton, not jeans or sweats. The smock had the logo for the store and café, and Pop and Gram felt it gave a consistent look for all employees to wear one.

Kay had been on vacation, so this was the first Maude was seeing her on this visit. "Hi! I was hoping I'd see you soon!"

The smile on Kay's face lit up the room. She looked at Maude and said, "So . . . what's new?" Then, she winked at Gram and then another wink at Pop.

"Well, we were just telling our granddaughter that you are about to teach her everything you know!" Pop said and playfully tapped Maude on the shoulder.

"Aha, yes, congrats on all of this, Maude. You're a good kid, and you'll do well. So, yes, I saw you come in and wanted to pop in and let you know when you're ready, I can show you a few things." Kay folded her hands in front of her and smiled warmly.

"Okiedokie. So, I think I'm ready," Maude said, glancing at Pop and Gram for approval.

"Yep, go ahead with Kay. We'll catch up with you in a bit," Gram said and walked over for a hug. As Maude neared the door, her stomach was nervous, and she glanced back at her grandparents. Pop made kissy lips and said, "Poo, poo, poo," imitating the sound of smooches.

She smiled, blew a kiss to he and Gram, and made her way to the front with Kay.

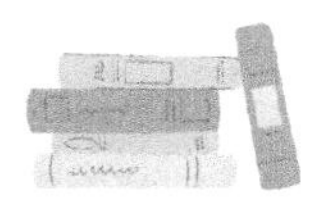

Kay and Maude sat at a table in the cafe with some folders, their drinks, and Kay's laptop open.

"Maudie, I'm so proud of you! You've blossomed into a beautiful and bright young woman. I have no doubt you can do this." Kay put her pen down and reached for Maude's hands. "The Lord is on your side. He always has been and always will be. I am full of confidence in this role for you. Of course, it is entirely your decision now and in the future, but please know I am here to help. Your grandparents are here, too, and we're not going to toss you into this blindfolded. You will get this all down, and you can count on me to guide you as long and as far as you need me," Kay said.

"Thank you so much," Maude responded. "If you're willing to help—even in the future when I'm lost on something—that's so appreciated." Maude smiled but quickly sipped her drink to avoid the tears begging to trickle out of the corner of her eyes.

"Yes, absolutely. But I think you'll recognize a lot of this through years of just . . . being here. You know? You may not have been scheduling or approving invoices, but you have been around to hear and see things. You have a good head on your shoulders. As much as your grandpa and grandma cherish you, if you were not accustomed to being here or aware of your surroundings, I don't think they'd have leaned on you for this. I think you'll pick up on things quickly and for those more challenging tasks, well, that's why we're here and will teach you," Kay said as she clicked and navigated through the laptop for files.

"Well, Pop and Gram have said they rely on you for your organizational skills." Maude chuckled and Kay smiled. "Clearly, they were right. Look at you with your color-coded and alphabetized folders!" She glanced at the laptop screen and saw many files laid out accordion-style.

"Thanks. It keeps things adequately at my fingertips, I guess. I printed this for you because it gives an overall view of the behind-the-scenes legal-type stuff we need for the company to thrive. For example, this spreadsheet has the names, timelines, codes, etc., of the various forms and such we use." Kay pulled out a plain brown clipboard with a handful of papers attached. An excel spreadsheet with an alphabetized list and dates and other factors lined up along the respective lines. "So this shows the day by day or week by week or quarterly—or whatever—form or timeframe we need to complete."

Maude read each line, realizing it all *seemed* straightforward. Fortunately, she was indeed fairly familiar with the lingo because of spending summers there and hearing and seeing how things worked, just as Kay had said. But actually seeing some of the paperwork for the first time and learning new ones, too, it felt manageable. Maybe it was Kay's kind words, but Maude didn't feel overwhelmed despite the amount of work she had no clue went into the business. Kay said trainings would continue, but in the meantime, she had to study and do her best to understand the ins and outs.

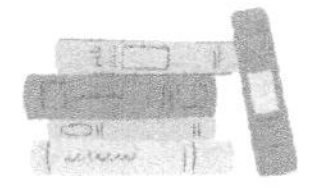

After a couple of hours, she went behind the counter for the first time as someone other than the granddaughter of the owners. She saw things she hadn't before. The shelf under the register had various business cards, loose-leaf paper, extension cords, and plugs. She saw a small box covered in dust far to the back behind some bigger boxers. She wondered if she should dig it out and saw no harm in giving the area a good dusting. The bigger boxes contained bookmarks, clip-on book lights, gift cards for each season, and various novelty items—all the things that appear in the check-out line. The small, off-white colored box was not labeled, and it wasn't taped or glued shut. She lifted the lid off the box and found a Bible, completely covered in dust and a little ripped. She was afraid it would crumble apart between her fingers. She probably shouldn't have, but she delicately flipped through the pages. She stopped flipping when an obstacle hindered her. It was a small, old, faded picture fit within the pages, used as a bookmark. Underlined in pencil was the verse, "By your wisdom and understanding you have gained wealth for yourself and amassed gold and silver in your treasuries" (Ezekiel 28:4).

She held the Bible closer to her face so she could see the old photo. She faintly saw a woman in a rocking chair, sewing. The chair was near a table with some things on it, though it was hard to make out what those things were. The woman's shirt had an unusual pattern—odd—not quite zig-zag lines, no particular order. It reminded Maude of her friend Rose's dishwasher where her little brother, a toddler, put his magnetic letters upside down and sideways and hanging off the edges. The lady in the photo was slouched in her chair and appeared to be in her nineties. Her hair was white and disheveled, and her dog, a Doberman, sat next to her.

Maude noticed Gram across the way smiling and headed her way. Maude froze, unsure if she should be ashamed for opening the box. She decided to ask about it.

"Gram, I just found this Bible buried way underneath the shelves here."

To her surprise, Gram was delighted.

"Oh, honey! You found it!" Gram lifted the Bible and flipped through the pages as delicately as Maude had. "Honey. I lost this. It's been missing for . . ." Her voice trailed off. "Here it is." Gram looked up and mouthed words, seeming to talk to God.

Maude could make out "photo" and "thank" although she didn't need to know more. It was obvious Gram was thanking God for locating these lost objects.

"This photo is a distant relative of mine from many generations ago. This was her Bible, and somehow, I misplaced it."

Tears welled up in her eyes. Maude's heart ached to see Gram cry.

"Gram. Oh my gosh, don't cry."

She hugged Gram tightly and buried her head onto Gram's shoulder. "You okay? I didn't mean to stir up all these emotions." She rubbed Gram's shoulder. "Can I get you anything?" Maude wracked her mind for a way to show Gram her love.

"Honey, it's okay. You've made my day. This was under the counter? Oh, look how dusty it is. My goodness. This Bible should not be handled. Look at me fiddling with it." She placed it gently on the counter. "It's so old; I'm afraid it'll fall apart. But, honey, this photo! This photo was from the Civil War era. My grandma gave it to me." Gram stared at the picture as she spoke.

"This is wonderful, Gram. It was under the shelf but really

far back. Are you okay? This is emotional stuff!" Maude once again rubbed Gram's arm affectionately.

"Let's get this Bible put back in the box . . . the photo too," Gram said as a tear trickled down her cheek. She smiled reassuringly. "Thank you, honey. This picture is my family. Someday this will be yours." Gram hugged Maude after bundling the photo and Bible back into the box and placed it near the ledge of the shelf, under the register.

Kay came over with a customer, so Gram and Maude shuffled out of the way. Gram went about working, and Maude didn't want to pry. She knew it must have been extraordinary for Gram to see the Bible and photo again. So, to give adequate time to process everything, Maude made her way to the storage room to unpack a new shipment and get the products marked and ready to be shelved.

Chapter Two

When Maude visited her grandparents, the quieter, softer ways of Ardendale appealed to her. At her dad's house near the city, she had grown used to the traffic and noise. However, the difference between there and Ardendale was night and day. A stroll around Ardendale was welcoming with the countryside, picturesque views, and a calm atmosphere. She walked down the street with Copper, listening to the pat-pat sound of her shoes echo off the sidewalk and leaves fluttering off of cars as they danced from the trees. The walks were refreshing. She and Copper rounded the corner from Spruce Street to Main Street. Main Street spanned only a few miles, but it had an impressive lineup of stores, restaurants, and businesses. The nearest big city, Benton, was fifty miles away.

In an effort to keep the town standing, the multi-million-dollar company, Schneider Construction LLC, had recently renovated all of Ardendale's infrastructure. The company was a wealthy conglomerate that built and restructured businesses. A large supercenter replaced two small grocery stores. A park was constructed, the medical building moved to a new facility, and several small shops were updated with some new stores sprinkled in. The plaza where Johnny had cut hair for forty years and Stella had done nails for twenty-five years was rebuilt. The insurance company building had a facelift. The furniture store was gutted and then rebuilt. Every owner was offered the ability to allow employees to keep their jobs. Not everyone was happy with the changes. Mom and Pop stores were no longer family-owned and operated, and *the way things used to be* had changed. However, the former structures no longer met building code specifications, and frankly, some of the older areas smelled moldy and wet. The owners didn't have the funds, energy, or desire to make the massive renovations. In this time of updates and attractive visual changes, many new families had moved in, something this town hadn't seen in a quarter-century.

A few miles behind Main Street stood acres upon acres of extra, hilly woods. Ardendale was an authentic country town when sometimes a bear or deer gallivanted around late at night. Behind the high school were woods, and the athletes often saw deer off in the distance. Most of the population lived right in town on one of a dozen streets that all ran directly into Main Street: Lancaster, Crown, Wright, River, Piper, and Front Street were streets with dozens of houses on each. The outskirts of town had farmland and a river that curved through it. Families that lived out that way were bussed in for school. Everyone knew where everyone lived and who worked where. This town was so small that others usually either knew everyone else's business, or more likely, thought they did. Though some people gossiped, most were truly friendly and genuinely committed to each other's best interests.

As Maude walked Copper down Main Street, people were mowing their lawns and watering plants. Some were sweeping the sidewalks in front of their stores. Two guys were working outside at the gas station, one using a squeegee on the windows and the other spraying down the blacktop around the gas pumps. A horn beeped in the distance. An older man whistled as he emerged from the flower shop with a bouquet of red carnations. He opened the passenger door to his car, laid the flowers on the front seat, shut the door, and walked around to climb behind the wheel. These personal moments made Maude happy. The slower pace of Ardendale allowed her to see details she didn't get to see back home.

Midway down Main Street, Copper pulled ahead. For safety, Maude kept her on a leash during walks. Suddenly, her tugging got harder, and Maude lost her footing. She skidded to a halt when she landed on her hands and knees on the gravel. "Copper! Ouch!" she yelled. Copper took off in a run straight ahead then veered to the left through an alley and out of sight. Maude hopped up and ran to see what was on the other side. There were cigarette butts and ankle-high grass, and the ground was squishy as she made her way through the debris. The beautiful brown brick-layered Bible Church was behind it, surrounded by nothing but pine trees and woods. She yelled for Copper again, but her voice only echoed. There were no cars or signs of people in the church parking lot. She ran around looking for open doors or hiding places but saw none, so she headed off to the edge of the woods just behind the church. It was full of pine needles and went uphill. She ran up the small knoll into a woodsier area with taller, older trees.

The leaves crinkled and crunched under her feet. She tracked on and continued to yell for Copper. Maude got scared when the church went out of sight, and light from town faded in the shade of the trees. She thought of Pop and Gram's sadness if they found out Copper was lost. She decided against calling her dad because she needed immediate help. The only other contact in town she had was Ned, her dad's best friend growing up. She memorized his number as a child in case of an emergency. She still knew it by heart. *It's funny how some things are unforgettable,* she thought to herself.

She dug her phone out of her pocket and dialed Ned. An

awful siren-type noise and robotic woman's voice answered. "We're sorry. The number you've . . ." She angrily hit the *end* button. "Stupid area code!" She dialed correctly the second time. Ned answered on the second ring.

"Hello?" He sounded confused.

"Ned? Hi, this is Maude, William's daughter. I'm in town visiting my grandparents, and their dog ran away. Can you help me? I'm behind the Bible Church in the woods." She chattered without stopping.

"Hi, Maude. Gosh. Yes. Um . . . Stay where you are. How far out are you? Don't go any further without me."

Ned said he was going to bring flashlights and come right away. In the meantime, Maude repeatedly yelled for Copper and took a few paces in the furthest direction. Tears welled up in her eyes, and her stomach churned to think of what a disappointment this would be to her grandparents. Finally, she collapsed to the ground with worry. "Copper!!" She lifted her head and yelled so loudly; her voice cracked. Occasionally she stood up and took a few paces and yelled more, but she didn't dare get herself lost. Besides, she told Ned she was just within sight of the town. If she moved, she'd be wasting his time trying to find her while Copper got further away.

Suddenly, she heard leaves rustling in the distance. She sprang up to look around. A dog barked, and leaves rustled. *Could it be Copper?* She twisted her head in all directions to search for the location of the sound. Suddenly, Ned's voice boomed. "Maude? It's Ned. Are you over here?"

She couldn't see him yet but knew he was just over the site of the knoll. When he came into sight, she ran toward him. Ned was about her dad's height, though much heavier and balding. He was wearing jeans, a faded sweatshirt, and gloves poked out of his side pockets. She felt instant relief to see her dad's dear friend, her "pseudo uncle."

"Ned, thank God! Did you just hear . . ." She began but her

voice trailed off when she saw a dog with Ned. Obviously, his German shepherd had barked, not Copper.

Together they tracked further into the woods. Ned's dog, Jazz, sniffed at Maude's clothes, hoping to trail Copper's scent left on her clothing. Maude had spent time with Ned and his family periodically through the years, so small talk was easy. Ned did most the talking, reassuring her that they'd find Copper. He asked her about her dad's company and told her about his own family business. The Morgan's were the owners of The Square Meal Diner in town. They were good business people who were in tune with their customers in a friendly, professional, and prayerful manner. They, no doubt, heard town gossip, but they didn't get involved. On the contrary, they treated their customers to inspirational, framed quotes on the walls, motivational quotes on the tables, and prayers whenever requested. The Morgan's were faithful people, and being a Christian herself, she always respected them.

It seemed like hours went by as they walked on deeper into the woods. Finally, Jazz barked and picked up speed. Ned's eyes lit up with hope. Maude took off in a run after Jazz, side by side with Ned. Not far along, Copper was happily resting inside an old stone foundation. Broken and weathered boards laid on the ground, and a set of bluestone steps led up from the foundation wall. There were traces of broken cement, and a single line of piping ran through the center, but the tubing was breaking apart. Copper was nestled in one corner, asleep. Jazz's bark woke her, and they stared at each other, seeming to communicate. *Thank God Copper was okay!* Maude didn't even notice the tears fall down her face when she ran down the steps into the foundation, and she knelt to squeeze Copper lovingly. Copper nestled her head near Maude's neck, and Maude gently petted Copper's back, silently saying a prayer of thanks. Maude then grabbed Copper's leash and stood up but stayed next to Copper.

"Hey there, Copper girl," Ned said, soothingly petting her

head as he stepped down into the mysterious large square near Maude. Copper was sitting up near where the pipes were breaking. Despite the dirt, cold cement, and rusty piping, she seemed peaceful, as though she'd taken a long, leisurely nap. Jazz was several feet back, smelling around in the woods. "She doesn't appear to be injured. Did you stop to rest, girl?" Ned asked, petting her again. Copper stood up, and when she did, they saw that she'd dug up a small hole near the broken pipe and several items were laying underneath her. Ned leaned down to investigate further.

Maude walked out of the foundation, keeping a close eye on Copper.

"Hey, Copper! Come on out of there. Come on, girl! Up we go. There. Good girl."

Maude spoke as she gently tugged on the leash to pull the dog up. This time, she wrapped the strap around her arm several times. She would not let her get away again.

"Maude, these items. They're . . . I mean they appear to be coins," Ned said, haltingly. Maude was squatting down petting Copper. "I think we should give these to the Historical Society. The question is, where did Copper find them?"

He walked back over to eye the foundation. Maude didn't say anything, absorbing the information. Ned walked back over to her as he turned the objects over repeatedly in his hands. She noticed he had put his gloves on.

"Coins? As in pennies?" she asked.

"Actually, these are not pennies. They're . . . I think . . . gold coins?" Ned said with a question in his voice. He brushed the dirt off the coins with his gloved fingers and blew on them. He lifted one just above eye level and squinted in the sunlight as he turned the coins repeatedly to look more closely.

"Wait. Gold? That can't be right. Why would there be *gold anything* in the woods? Who owns these woods and that foundation?" Maude nodded in the direction of the bluestone steps. "It appears to be massively old. I mean, are we allowed to take them, whatever they are?" she asked, looking at him. "Gloves? Why do you have gloves with you?" She smiled, in spite of the situation.

Ned chuckled. "I was fixing the siding on the diner when you called. I mean, now that I think about it, I guess I have them with me a lot just to take care of this and that around the restaurant. But I don't think we should touch these with our bare hands." He nodded at the coins. "The woods extend out beyond city limits. There isn't much upkeep needed. The foundation is as much a mystery to me as it is to you. I don't know for sure the proper etiquette for something like this, but Gabriel at the Historical Society will get to the bottom of it. It'll all be okay. And don't worry, I won't tell Philly and Marguerite about Copper," Ned said with a smile that reassured her.

Chapter Three

By the time she got home, Pop and Gram were at work, so she had the house to herself. She fed Copper and gave her plenty of water. Then Maude decided to de-stress as best she could. As she made her way to her bedroom, she thought about how the house was far larger than what they needed. Three bedrooms were scattered throughout the 2,200 square-foot home. Philly and Marguerite's room was on the east end, and two guest rooms were on the west end. Maude's room was actually meant to be a second family space because it had a screened porch and glass doors leading from it. Her dad used it as his bedroom growing up. The walls were plain white with burgundy curtains hanging above the glass doors. Pop and Gram bought those curtains for her to make the room more *girlish*. The third bedroom across the hall was smaller and used mostly as an office, with a futon and dresser in there. A full bath sat at the end of the hallway. Pop and Gram's bedroom had a full bath attached so though Maude's room was larger, they preferred theirs. The main living area separated the ends of the house, so the "guest" wing and "master" wing were reminiscent of wings.

She sat sideways on the swing inside the screened room and

put her feet up. The swing was striped beige and dark blue with a cover overhead. She nestled in with a neck pillow and listened to the sound of the tag on the underside of the swing flicking in the wind. Without meaning to, she fell asleep while the breeze tossed her hair. The noise of a door shutting woke her up, and she glanced far to the left to see Ned emerging from his Chrysler Sebring and heading toward the front door. She grabbed her phone and ran to the kitchen to let him in. Ned was her dad's eyes and ears when it came to her grandparents and the store, so he had a house key to use just in case no one was home.

"Hi, Ned! I was just trying to regroup after the incident today," Maude said while glancing at her phone and suddenly realizing she had missed a call from him. "Sorry again for today," she apologized.

"It is not your fault. No problem! I still can't believe Copper took off like that," Ned commented, looking over at Copper sound asleep in her bed. "I called you earlier—hope it's okay to come by. I knew your grandparents would be at the store, and I want to touch base with you about the coins. I left them with Gabriel. He is an historian, so he'll be able to guide you further." He reached into his back pocket, removed his wallet, took out a business card, and handed it to her. "Here is his info. I told him what happened and he's a good man. He'll keep it quiet."

"Awesome, thank you. I'll give him a call in a while," Maude said. "The coins, Copper running off, it's all surreal."

"It definitely was out of character for Copper. I trust Gabriel, though. He is a noble man, and if anyone can get to the bottom of this, it's him," Ned said as he walked toward the door. "You okay? Do you need anything else?" he asked Maude.

"Thanks again, Ned. I'm okay. We will see what Gabriel figures out. Seriously, thank you. It was such a relief to have your help today, and now this. Just, thank you." She reached up to embrace him.

"It's all going to be okay, Maudie," Ned said. Maude smiled at the sound of her nickname. "I have to head out now, but let me know if you need anything else." He opened the door to leave.

"Thanks again. See you soon," Maude replied. Ned let himself out, and she headed to the refrigerator to get something for lunch. After making a bologna sandwich and watching Gram's favorite show, *The Young & the Restless,* while she ate, Maude was able to think more clearly. She dialed Gabriel and got his voicemail. She left a detailed message as his voicemail had instructed, then decided to call her dad. He was just the person she could talk to about Ned, the dog, and the coins.

After her dad's line began to ring, it occurred to Maude that Ned may have already called him. "Maudie! Hello, my girl! How's Pop and Gram?" he answered enthusiastically. Maude spent the next few minutes filling him in on the walk, Copper, Ned, the coins and cracked foundation, and on the bookstore. Maude and her dad were close, so she knew he would have told her if he'd heard from Ned. "Okay. I was going to surprise you but . . . I am coming down tomorrow afternoon to spend a few days. We can get all this figured out when I get there." She felt butterflies when she heard her dad was coming. Missing him would be the only disadvantage of moving here permanently. They didn't see each other a ton between work and school, but when her mom died, they were all each other had. She didn't mind still living at home. He didn't pry. He made work his life. It didn't take away from taking care of Maude, but he hadn't dated or done much aside from work, seeing her school plays, and visiting Pop and Gram as much as he could.

Somehow, she missed Gabriel's return call. "Hi, Maude. This is Gabriel Titus. I am glad you called. Ned told me about your discovery. Come by tomorrow morning at nine if you're able. I'm on the third floor of the Beecher's Building, 2308 Main Street. The door is on the side. Ring the buzzer. I'll be waiting.

Okay, thanks. Bye." *Static.* "To delete this message . . ." The robotic woman's voice starting going through the options. Maude hung up. Nine would work fine tomorrow. She could fill her dad in later.

Maude decided not to tell Pop and Gram about Copper's trip into the woods. Later that evening, they enjoyed takeout from a local pizza place, and then Marguerite left to attend a Bible study at church. While Maude was invited to attend, she felt more tired than usual after the exhausting day and put on pajamas early in the evening. Philly was a baseball fan, and shortly after dinner, he relaxed in his blue recliner to watch a game and then dozed off to sleep almost immediately. So, it was easy for Maude to shield her emotions about almost losing Copper. As the night wore on, her blood pressure returned to normal.

By nine the next morning, Maude was in Gabriel's office. It was stacked with papers, and he joked it was his fish tank because the office had all-glass walls in the middle of a large, musty-smelling room. Gabriel only stood around 5'4" and had one spider web strand of hair on top of his head that danced in the wind of the ceiling fan. She smiled at the memory of attending an Easter service at the Bible Church one year when Gabriel, who is also the Reverend there, stood at the front with that same strand of hair floating around while he spoke. The memory stuck in her mind for some reason. Today he was wearing gray khakis and a white button-down shirt. He had a gaited walk and got right down to business.

"These coins are ancient," Gabriel said, flipping through some old newspapers and not looking at Maude when he spoke.

She took a seat in the chair just inside his office. Reading from somewhere, he said, "The Half Eagle, the $5.00 gold piece, was the very first gold denomination of any type minted by the United States. Congress first authorized it in 1792." Gabriel paused. "The coins you found appear to be from the tail end of the 1700s. I have never actually seen any of these up close and personal before. This is utterly amazing you've discovered them." She nodded. "Ned didn't give much info except that your dog got loose, and you found them somewhere outside of town in the woods. I'm afraid we should keep this quiet for now until we discover more."

"Absolutely, sir," Maude replied.

"Happy to help. Thanks for reaching out. I understand how word can spread, so thank you for your discretion. Best I keep the coins and get them cleaned up. I hope we're able to get to the bottom of this. Let me do some further investigating and get back to you." He smiled. "Tell your dad hello for me." He directed her toward the door. She thanked him and headed down the hall to the elevator.

Maude started toward her car when she saw a storefront across the street. Hamden's Emporium, the old-fashioned sign read. The window display was so dusty that cobwebs were visible from where she stood twenty-five yards away. There was an old rocking chair with an old guitar on top, and flat against the window was an overturned mannequin. The dress on the mannequin looked familiar. Where had she seen that pattern before? It reminded her of scattered letters in all sorts of directions. That was it! It was the photo inside her Gram's Bible! Could this be the same pattern? It had to be a coincidence. After she got close enough, she cupped her hand against the window to peer inside. What she could see was a mostly vacant room with opened boxes, dust, brooms, and a vacuum plugged into the front wall. The sign in the front door said, "Closed due to Big Business."

She walked over a few feet to peer closer at the pattern. It was identical to what she could remember of the photo. Curiosity got the best of her, and she walked right into the store. "Hello?" she called. Her footsteps creaked and echoed on the hardwood, terribly filthy floors.

"Hello, Miss. Can I help you?" An old voice coming from the back of the store startled her.

Before her stood an older man no more than five feet tall with dandruff on the shoulders of his dark blue polo shirt. His nose was pudgy, and he wore thin glasses on the bridge of his nose. His back was arched over enough that he appeared to be in pain as he walked. "Yes, hello. My name is Maude. I am the granddaughter of the local Lincoln family that owns The Books Are Here. My dad is William Lincoln." Maude searched his face for acknowledgment.

"Philly and Marguerite. Yes. I know them. I remember your dad too. Boy, I remember you skipping around town with your red hair ribbons and tap shoes as a little girl. It's good to see you again." The older man's face brightened.

"Thanks. I'm sorry. Are you completely closed? Something I saw in your front window captured my attention. I am curious about it." She took a nervous step toward him.

He put out his hand out to shake hers. "Name is Tommy Hamden. The *corporation* came in and took over everything. My store needs real repairs, and I haven't the means or family to do it anymore. They've offered to buy me out, and I've had no choice but to accept. I'm just cleaning up here and selling whatever I have left. I'm happy to show you whatever it is you'd like." He stepped toward the window.

"Oh, thank you, sir," Maude replied. She headed to the window. "This rocking chair is in great shape. I'm looking for one to have at my grandparent's house." She wanted to get closer to the dress before she asked any questions about it. They walked over to the display, and he picked up the mannequin. *It had to be the same pattern!* "I'm also wondering about this dress. It is unique, isn't it? This pattern reminds me of a dress my, eerr, my grandma used to wear," she lied.

He nodded his head. "We've had this rocking chair for as long as I can remember. It was here when I inherited this store. The dress, though, isn't a cloth for dresses; it is drapery material. It is about a quarter of the price of dress cloth. I have never sold a yard of this material since I inherited this business." He turned away, commenting, "Follow me, dear." He led them to the back corner of the store, moved a ladder into position, and started to climb it. From the top shelf, he pulled down a great cob of dust balls and a box. He cracked it open, and an overpowering smell of mothballs barreled out. Inside was a bundle of the same pattern material. "Here, you can have this or the dress. Actually, take the rocking chair too. I have no use for them now that I've lost my store." Maude's heart broke for him.

"I'd love to keep these things, sir. I'll take good care of them for you." She meant it. She looked around some more in hopes of helping him feel less lonely. She listened to him vent about *big business* taking over. She offered him empathy, but her mind was busy thinking about the material. She wasn't sure what to do with any of the information but felt fortunate to discover it, nonetheless. She left him some money, despite his protests, and then needed two trips to get the goods outside. Her car was a hatchback, so everything fit when she collapsed the seats. He gave her an old business card just for good measure.

Chapter Four

The next morning at The Books Are Here, Maude was filing some of the store's business papers as moms and grandmas pushing strollers started to file in. They carried bulky diapers bags, babies on hips, and had talkative or crying kids in tow. Two mornings a week, there was storytime in the children's section at The Books Are Here. It was always packed, regardless of the weather or other events going on in Ardendale.

Maude continued doing paperwork, trying to learn the ins and outs of the business, but she couldn't help but be curious about storytime. She made her way to the back of the store to the children's section. The bright sound of children's chatter echoed the closer she got. She peeked in to see about three dozen people scattered through the many different children's area sections. The stage for storytime was set up on the right side while on the opposite side was an area that had a train table and toys set out to play with. During storytime, there was almost always a craft or take-home activity associated with the story available, and today that table was parallel to the stage.

A woman leaning against the craft table looked familiar. She had caramel-highlighted brown hair, was thin and of tall stature, with stunning brown eyes. It seemed like she had exquisite taste in clothing and shoes. Maude suddenly realized it was Ned's wife, Lucy.

In front of Lucy crawled a little girl who looked to be about six months old. She had a heart-shaped face with a wide forehead and a pointed chin laced with drool that shined when it caught the store lights. Her eyes were a piercing, icy blue, and she had the longest eyelashes Maude had ever seen. Her nose was slightly up-turned, and her mouth had one single baby tooth poking out of her upper gums. Her hair was baby fine, yellow as the sun, with a pink barrette falling out of the ponytail on top of her head. Her little legs and arms were full of chub rolls, and her plain pink dress fell just over the edge of her white diaper cover. She wore matching pink shoes with frills on the top. Her nearly toothless grin accentuated her adorableness as she beamed at the storyteller who was smiling back at her.

"Oh, Rosalie. You have the workers smitten just like the rest of us," Lucy said to her granddaughter as she leaned down to kiss the top of the baby's head.

The reader smiled at Lucy then looked back at the baby. "She sure does! What a beauty!" Maude recognized Victoria as today's reader. She was in her early 50s, though she appeared to be in her 30s with her long, curly blond hair. She stood about 5'5" and had a medium build. Victoria had a warm disposition and always treated Maude with respect. The grandma smiled a proud grin and pulled Rosalie back to her lap, handed her a Winnie the Pooh rattle, and whispered in the baby's ear. In her left hand was a bottle at the ready. Parents and grandmothers began to take their seats on the floor in front of the stage. Maude couldn't help but stifle a laugh when the majority of them groaned when kneeling. She heard a few say, "I'll never get back up," while others nodded and chose to stand. With that, storytime began, and Maude walked back toward the front of the store.

As she neared the United Stated History section, suddenly Maude heard a thud and then a clunk in the aisle. She rushed over to see an older gentleman in his sixties getting onto his knees from a horizontal position. He saw her and, as quickly as he could, shot back up again. "My apologies, ma'am, I seem to have lost my footing. I'm just fine." Before she could say anything, he teeter-tottered slightly on his feet. He was able to catch himself by grabbing a shelf. But it was clear from the sweat on his brow and his pale skin that he was ill.

"Sir, I think it'd be a good idea to call for help. It appears you are feeling dizzy. Is there someone I can call for you?" Maude asked as she grabbed a sturdy, brown wooden chair that was just at the end of the aisle. He sat down on it as he reached into his right pocket to grab a white handkerchief. It had 'B.C.P.' monogrammed in blue on it. He used it to wipe his forehead as he exhaled deeply. "Can I get you some water?" She reached for the walkie-talkie on her belt to have The AM to PM Cafe bring him something. "Cafe?" She tried to remember who was working in the cafe. *Faith, that was right.* "Hey, Faith? I need water in the US History aisle. Someone isn't feeling well," she said in a low but urgent voice into the walkie-talkie.

Static. "Maude? Okay, be right there." Faith's gentle voice came through the walkie-talkie.

She pulled up a second chair that was close to where the other one had been and took a seat next to him. "What's your name?" she asked him.

He continued to wipe his forehead. She instinctively knew to call an ambulance. "Sir, I'd like to call for an ambulance. Maybe they'll help you to feel better." She tried to sound calm.

"I have been experiencing issues with my blood sugar, honey.

I know what is wrong. But that's fine. My wife, can you call her too?" He reached for his cell phone, clipped to his pocket in a black carry case. "Shirley is her name." He leaned his head back and rested it against the books behind him.

Maude called for an ambulance, and they said they would be right there. Then she called his wife, whose voice was unsteady when she heard her husband wasn't feeling well. "Oh, Bernie. His blood sugar was low this morning, but I had my hair appointment over at Shirley's, so I wasn't there to keep track of him. Oh, dear. What can I do? Should I come there?"

Maude reassured her the ambulance was on their way, and she'd stay with him. She offered to call Shirley back with an update once the ambulance arrived, but Shirley insisted she'd come to the store. Maude sat right next to Bernie and made small talk with him until the ambulance arrived. In a short few minutes, two gentlemen wheeled in a stretcher and asked Maude and Bernie what happened. While Maude answered all their questions thoroughly, she couldn't help but notice the one EMT. He appeared to be in his mid-20s with green eyes and long eyelashes. He had a round face with nicely tanned skin, offset by his white EMT uniform. His lips were thin, and he had deep dimples on his cheeks. His hair was dark brown and buzzed short. He was muscular, had no facial hair, and was simply handsome. His nametag read "Marc," and she thought he actually did look like a "Marc."

Maude quickly turned away, embarrassed to be attracted to an EMT in a situation like this—*so cliché,* she thought. She internally scolded herself and focused back on Bernie, who was now laying down on the stretcher with oxygen under his nose.

When Marc spoke, his voice was deep and just as beautiful as he was. "Maude. You did a great job keeping the situation calm," he said while smiling at her.

She realized he must have seen her nametag. *I can't believe this nametag my grandparents made for me for fun as a kid is legit.* "Thanks. I did my best. Can I do anything more to help?"

"We may need to reach you later for more details, but we have what we need for now," he replied as his counterpart put a light blanket over Bernie's legs. Bernie's color was returning to normal just as Shirley walked up.

"Bernie. There you are. Here is your snack," Shirley said. But as she went to hand it to him, the other EMT stopped her.

"Hello, Ma'am. We'll need to wait before we give him any food. Are you his wife?" The EMT, whose nametag said, "Ken," told Shirley.

"Yes, I am. Whatever you need to do. We appreciate your service. Do you need to take Bernie with you?" Shirley asked in a calm voice.

"Yes. We'll take him to Benston Hospital unless you have another preference." Ken began to wheel Bernie out. Marc followed. Suddenly, Marc turned to Maude, and she was embarrassed to feel butterflies when he did.

"Hey. Thanks again for your help. I haven't seen you around here before. It's nice to meet you." Marc smiled at her.

"Thanks. I actually think I will be living here. This is my grandparents' store. I'm supposed to take it over." Marc continued to smile. "There isn't much keeping me back home, and I'm the only one who can take over here." She realized she was rambling and felt silly. "So, yes, I will be living here. I'm Liam Lincoln's daughter." She quickly finished talking, aware that Bernie would need Marc's attention and he'd need to leave.

Marc nodded. "Ah, okay. I've heard of your dad. And your grandparents? Incredible people." He paused as if waiting for her response. "Okay, I'll . . . we'll be in touch. Thanks, Maude," he said as he glanced outside as if to signal he was on his way.

"Okay. Hope Bernie is okay. Happy to help." She glanced down at the counter and brushed away some invisible dust. He waved as he pushed open the doors and left.

When she got home later that day, she was over the moon excited to see a rental car parked in the driveway. Knowing it must be her dad's car, she took off in a run for the front door. As she got closer, she heard his voice in the kitchen. She squealed with excitement, ripped open the screen door, and jetted into the kitchen. Not sure if her feet were even touching the ground, she leapt to her dad.

"Maudie!" He hugged her and kissed the top of her head. He was 6' 2" and thin, with a sharp chin, pointy nose, and combed over short, salt and pepper hair that covered his tall forehead. He had on khaki tan shorts with a plain dark blue pullover. Pop was to his left in his standard gray overalls and a white button-down shirt. Pop used to be 5'11" but was getting a little shorter each year as people often do the older they get. He was smiling at their embrace.

"Dad! I'm so glad you're here!" Maude shouted, realizing how much she missed him. She supposed that knowing she was most likely in Ardendale to stay, seeing her dad was extra special. For the first time, she felt sad and a little homesick. Her lip was trembling, which made her feel foolish. "I would have picked you up at the airport. How was your flight?" she asked while squeezing him tight again.

"All smooth. I knew you were working, and besides, I knew Pop and Gram would be making their famous goulash, so I wanted to get here!" He looked over at Gram, who Maude hadn't even realized was in the kitchen. She'd been so focused on her dad; she hadn't paid any attention to her or the incredible smell of meat and spices wafting through the house.

Pop moved over to the stove and leaned down to smell the concoction. Gram was wearing a floral apron, and she had a seashell necklace on that Maude remembered making for her as a child. Gram stirred the goulash as Pop walked back over to Maude and her dad. "Our family all together. Nothing gets better than this!" Pop said as he clapped his hands and pulled out chairs so everyone could sit. Everyone circled together at the kitchen table, took their seats, and casually chatted.

Dad talked about work in the way he usually did by saying, "busy, busy!" Pop and Gram talked about business at The Books Are Here and continually looked over at Maude to include her. She had a few thoughts and occasionally chimed in, such as how to improve storytime, small details regarding a few financial statements she had learned about, and even a thing or two about the cafe. She sounded confident in her knowledge, and if she was honest with herself, she was feeling good about . . . everything.

"You young minds," Gram said affectionately, reaching over to touch Maude's hand. "Your young brain is picking things up so quickly! We are impressed that you've caught on so quickly. You seem to be enjoying yourself too. Are you feeling okay about things, Maude?" she asked. Maude blushed. Gram must have noticed because she quickly reached forward to grab her hand. "Sorry to put you on the spot, honey. Just know we're proud of the interest you're taking and the work you've been doing." Gram resqueezed Maude's hand and smiled at her.

Maude knew how important this was to Pop and Gram. Knowing this was a safe place with her family there, she used the opportunity to discuss the subject a little more. "I like it all. I guess I'm a perfectionist, so I'm taking on a lot of the paperwork in an effort to get ahead. Kay has been great. She is more than happy to show me the ins and outs." She paused to take a drink of her lemonade. "Seriously, her kindness and patience radiates from the inside out. I don't sense much opposition, you know, the *Oh, give the job to your granddaughter* people. In fact, 99% of the employees have been helpful. The respect the employees have for you guys is clear that they are loyal people. Kay echoed what you said about things being in great shape given the state of some of the village shops rebuilding or selling. It seems you guys have weathered the storm," she contributed, although her voice was shaky as she spoke. *I'm so corny!* Maude thought.

"That's nice of you to say to Pop and Gram, Maudie. I think you should know something about the business. It's nothing bad; it's just something that never came up." William paused to read Maude's face. "The reason for the great condition of the store compared to other stores in Ardendale is because, through the years, I've been happy to . . . no, I've been *privileged* to help to keep the store in a thriving condition, updating and modernizing as much as possible." He smiled from his mom to his dad. The look on his face was genuine, no ego attached. Maude knew her dad's looks—stern, honest, fierce (when ego-driven), and loving. He was even-tempered and honest. In his work-life, he paid allegiance to his clients, and career-driven as he naturally was, he was anxious to do his best. And when it came to family, he was genuine and loyal.

Maude noticed a gentle tear of pride welling up on Gram's face. Her dad was an only child, and that meant honoring his parents. It spoke volumes that he gave freely to Pop and Gram. She was willing to bet The Books Are Here could be the most up-to-date store in town, though she couldn't say for sure. She had been in Ardendale's Public Library a few times and remembered it having an adequate supply of books, but now that she thought about it, Pop and Gram's store was much more modern and well-equipped.

Suddenly, Maude's breath caught in her chest when she realized the undertaking running the store would mean. The circle of loyal employees, financial patterns, appliances, supplies—not just books—were all crucial to its success. The bigger picture, the behind-the-scenes details, and the legacy—it made her anxious but motivated to work that much harder to honor Pop and Gram's legacy.

Chapter Five

When morning arrived, Maude woke feeling nostalgic. She dreamed she was in a park surrounded by lilac bushes with her mom and dad. Though she didn't know where the park was supposed to be located, there was a fair going on with a red, white, and blue ferris wheel, balloon animals and game booths, and a few roller coasters sprinkled in between. Maude's images of her mom mostly came from photos since she was too young to truly remember her, but fortunately, her dad had hundreds of photos Maude frequently looked through. After pleasantly remembering the dream, she walked over to the fireplace mantel, which had a set of shelves mounted nearby. On the second shelf was an album of pictures of her mom, Hazel, and Maude and Liam. There were many pictures of the three of them in the hospital just after Maude was born and in those first few weeks at home. Maude's grandparents cherished their daughter-in-law Hazel, and the loss was just as difficult for them as it would have been on Hazel's parents had they not already passed prior to her death in a tragic car accident when Hazel was eighteen. Hazel had inherited their house but sold it a few years later when she and Liam got married and wanted a newer home with more room. Maude shuddered at the tragedy her mom's family had gone through. She realized she was lucky to have her dad, her grandparents, and a future to look forward to.

Liam's footsteps creaked as he walked down the hallway into the kitchen. Pop and Gram had made arrangements to work just the morning so they could then spend the rest of the day with Maude and Liam. Maude made her way to the kitchen, where her dad was pouring coffee into a plain white mug. "Hey, Maudie. Sleep good, sweetie?" He yawned as he put the pot back on the burner.

"Yep! Actually, I dreamt about you and me and Mom going to a fair." Maude searched her dad's face for emotion, realizing she didn't think before she shared. She never felt afraid to talk about her mom, but she didn't do it too often, not wanting to remind her dad of the terrible loss. From what Maude knew of her mom, she was a brilliant, beautiful soul. She'd never heard a single bad thing about her. If she was as wonderful as people said, then it must have been even more horrible for Liam to lose her.

"We took you to a fair when you were two. You were a bit young, but the stuffed animals and balloons had you mesmerized!" He looked off to the right and smiled, remembering something. "You know, I know we have never really talked about your mom's death." He walked over to sit down at the table. "I shut down." He took a sip of his drink. "When I lost the love of my life and you lost your mother at four—it was devastating. Needless to say, I didn't handle things perfectly. I'm sorry." The silence permeated the room. "But you are perfect. Despite my mistakes, you turned out to be intelligent, empathetic, street smart, and perhaps a new business owner?" He grinned at her. Maude smiled back.

"Dad, I am sure you did the best that you could. And thank you. I learned it all from you!" Maude had more she wanted to ask, like if he was happy, if work truly fulfilled him, if being so career-driven was worth it. But she didn't want to pry. She and her dad were alike in that sense.

Before he could respond, his pocket rang. He reached into it for his cell phone. "Ah, it's Ned." He looked at the screen and tapped it before placing it to his right ear. "Hey, buddy. Good. Yep. Okay, so, say ten at the church?" He looked at the wall clock and Maude. She nodded, remembering they had made plans to visit the foundation in the woods today that Copper had run off to. "Yep, see you then. Thanks. Bye."

"We're meeting Ned at the Bible Church at ten to head out. Gabriel is going with us. I told Mom and Dad we'd be spending father-daughter time and would even bring Copper with us," he said as he took a sip of his black coffee.

"Okiedokie. Let me get ready then," Maude said. She walked over to the cupboard to grab a protein bar, poured herself a glass of orange juice, and walked to her bedroom.

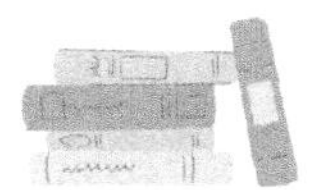

At ten sharp, Liam and Maude pulled into the Bible Church parking lot. Gabriel and Ned were standing near the church entrance with Ned's dog, Jazz. Copper barked from the back seat when she saw Jazz. "Dog talk, I suppose," Liam commented, rubbing Copper's head after he hooked a dark green leash onto Copper's neck collar. Jazz also was on a leash.

After exchanging hellos, the group of four, plus two dogs, began their hike. Before they were over the initial knoll, Gabriel spoke. "Unfortunately, I was unable to do the full amount of research this requires, but the time I had was put to good use. From what I have found, these coins appear to be the real thing. If, indeed, they are gold coins that are worth more money than this town is worth, I'm afraid we will need to hand all evidence over to Marian." He paused. "I assume you know who I'm talking about," Gabriel said, looking over at Maude to address her. "Marian McCarthy is the local legal eagle here. Everyone knows her, and she knows the ins and outs of this town. She would potentially have to determine the legal ramifications of the findings and who, if any one person in particular, the money belongs to. I can research to shorten her case, but that's the best I can do." They climbed a few minutes in silence, taking in the surroundings.

"What if they're not worth anything? Or even a small amount? What then?" Maude asked, breaking the silence.

"Small amounts get filed under the 'Finders Keepers' laws. Beyond that, things need to be reported to the authorities," he said.

"Authorities?" Maude asked.

He continued, "It is one thing if you'd been alone and found the coins and hadn't told anyone. In that case, chances are no one would know, and you could have cashed the coins in out of town, and Ardendale would have been out of the loop. But since we are all involved, if they are worth a lot, we have to give them over. But I think the bigger question is, how did these gold coins get there? What is the story behind it? As an historian, this is *fascinating* to me, and I'm anxious to see the foundation and to investigate." Gabriel smiled and rendered a chuckle.

"I remember something," Liam said. Everyone looked at him. "My dad and I came out here when I was a kid. I remember him telling me there was land out here that Mom's family used to own. The Dobermans we had growing up were all bred from the same family, and I feel like the original house was here," Liam looked around. "It's fuzzy in my memory. I can't recall the exact details. But I knew the story about where we got the dogs, and no, wait, maybe it was land elsewhere. I wish I could remember more. I was so young."

"Did you come here with Pop just that once, Dad?" Maude asked him.

"Once. Then, when I was a teenager, I was up here with some buddies, partying." Liam looked over at Ned, and Ned chuckled.

"Dad!" Maude exclaimed.

"Oh, now it was pretty straightforward. A bunch of my buddies and me hanging out, celebrating the end of school. We weren't more than fifty yards up," Liam said. "Good times."

"Where has the time gone?" Ned asked, looking blankly into the distance.

"How much further do we have to go?" Gabriel asked. He appeared to be in good physical shape despite his age, so it never occurred to Maude to be concerned about him going deep into the woods. He kept up with the rest of them.

Ned responded. "We must have been at least a couple of miles in. I'd say we have maybe another mile or so to go. Maybe? The bigger challenge is finding the exact spot. It wasn't a straight line exactly. Jazz and Copper should be able to guide us. But I think I'll recognize it as we get closer. Maude, do you recognize anything yet?"

She spun around 360 degrees. "I remember seeing some trees with X's on them. Who knows why? But I think when we see an area without trees nearby, we'll know we're close." She looked around at everybody.

Before anyone said another word, Copper and Jazz simultaneously barked. Their ears shot up, and they yanked on Liam and Ned's arms, jerking the men forward. "Whoa, Jazzy girl! We're alright," Ned said, patting Jazz's head. But the dogs were yanking the leashes. "It's this way." He nodded ahead. "Good girls!"

They walked along, following the dogs' lead. Just when Maude thought they were never going to find the foundation again, the dogs would sniff and bark and give her hope. As she looked around and saw no part of Ardendale in the distance, she grabbed hold of her dad's arm, glad to have several people in the party on this trip. The crunch of leaves and breaking twigs echoed as they tracked on. It seemed endless, but finally, the dogs seemed to know the way and led them directly to the foundation.

Like a child, Maude ran as soon as she spied it. Somehow the foundation appeared bigger this time. There was still the dirt and old stone stairs, but the edges seemed wider. Copper and Jazz immediately used their noses as guides as they ran around; the middle portion where the pipes were looked exactly as it had the other day. Copper used her paws to dig at the metal as Jazz barked at the pipes. Gabriel stood watching with a confused look on his face. "I'm not sure we should let the dogs dig like that. Were the pipes this way when you found them?" he asked, looking at Liam.

Liam shrugged his shoulders. "I wasn't here. I don't know."

Ned chimed in. "When we found Copper, the pipes were like this. Was Copper the one who uncovered them initially? Hard to tell. They were protruding out like that, but the dirt around it did seem to be newly moved. Jazz contributed to the mess, though."

"Well, I guess we can't do much to preserve this then. Let's pull the dogs out of there so we can do a walk around on foot," Liam said. But before he could stop the dogs, Copper and Jazz barked loudly, repeatedly. They spotted a rusted orange pipe with chipped brown pieces falling off. It was broken in half, and gold coins spilled out of the middle. The pipe had been hammered and crimped shut on the ends. It was a single pipe, maybe one foot long.

"That is not a sewer pipe! Look at those coins. Oh, my word," Gabriel said, making his way over to the foundation. Copper and Jazz kept digging with their paws and brought up four more pipes, making a total of five. Each was identical—

rusted, hammered, and crimped shut. All were about a foot long, but only one had broken in half. Everyone stood in silence, not sure what to make of the situation. Gabriel took latex gloves out of his back pocket, put them on, and picked up the rusted pipe in one hand, and the gold coins in the other hand. "Who would leave this kind of money here? These are in *mint condition*! Gang, these are gold pieces. Ned, can you put on those gloves I gave you? Then I need a bag; it's in my backpack." Ned obliged, and Gabriel put the coins in the bag and placed them on the edge of the foundation. "I am absolutely sure these are real gold coins. I suppose what I saw the other day had been handled too much and was too filthy to be sure. But these are definite."

"Are you saying these are legit gold coins?" Ned asked.

"I believe so. Did you say they were sitting in the dirt the other day?" Gabriel asked.

"When we found Copper, she was laying on top of the coins. The pipe was manipulated but not opened. When I handled the coins, I tried to keep my fingers just on the edges, but the dog had already been in contact with them for who knows how long." Ned squatted down to peer inside the bag of coins.

"I need another bag for these pipes," Gabriel stated. Liam grabbed one from the backpack. "I've never seen such a thing. This is unbelievable. I wouldn't have believed if I hadn't seen it with my own eyes." Gabriel shook his head as he looked from Maude to Ned in disbelief.

Maude stood speechless. It was all mysterious but also rather exciting. Her thoughts were interrupted with the sound of some siren blaring in the distance. Ned's phone made a chime but ended abruptly. He grabbed it out of its holder on his waist. "No reception. Sorry about that." But in town, the siren blared again, barely audible from this far out. Liam looked at Ned. Liam grabbed his phone but shook his head. "No reception for you, either? We're too far out. That sounds like the fire alarm in town. They must be paging me to come. Roger is there today, though, so hopefully it's nothing," Ned explained.

Gabriel, Liam, and Ned used sticks to dig around some more but did not find any more pipes. Maude sat under a tree nearby, giving the dogs some water. "Well, we have everything in bags, so I think that's about all we can do right now," Gabriel said as he walked out of the foundation.

"All right. Let's head back then," Ned said, and everyone obliged, gathering their things to begin the trek back.

It was silent for a few minutes as everyone considered the findings in the woods, and no one really knew what to make of what they had found. Liam broke the silence. "These were homes out here at one time, weren't there, Gabriel?" he asked.

"Yes. In the 1800s, people had what we'd now call homes out here. Back then, they didn't have the materials we use now. There wasn't adequate siding or insulation, but that's all anyone knew at the time. The town of Ardendale that we know now consisted of dirt roads, a few homes here and there, but this out here . . . was where most of the homes were. Around 1900, the current streets and homes replaced the ones out here. This area where we're standing eventually became woods, and I suppose these woods could be considered a sort of wall that separates our town from others. This really is what makes Ardendale so attractive to people—the beauty in all the land and rivers we have here. These woods are probably where wild animals come off the mountains, cross the highway, and settle in."

Liam laughed. "I remember people wanting to hunt out here, but it was too close to town and not allowed. My dad told me that. Here we are in the very woods the animals fled to."

"This time of year, these woods are quiet. We wouldn't want to come during hunting season or in the winter," Gabriel reasoned.

"I wonder if there'd be records of who lived out here. I swear some of my ancestors did live here," Liam said pointedly.

The siren sounded louder the closer they got to town. Ned rechecked his phone. "Ah, reception." He poked at his phone and put it to his ear. His face transformed with a look of fear as he listened to his voicemail. "The clerk's office is on fire! It's bad." He and Jazz began to jog, and everyone else followed. The smell of smoke slowly trickled into the woods, reminding Maude of a campfire, but without the pleasant memories one usually would have. When the wind blew, the smell got more intense, and Ned coughed. The sight of red and orange flames flickered in the distance. The sound of crackling, falling building pieces echoed, and panic ensued. Ned ran off as everyone neared the church parking lot. As he jumped into his car, he shouted: "Everyone head away from the fire. The smoke is dangerous. Liam, you guys should be okay at your parents' house but consider taking a drive if you'd prefer. Gabriel, get your wife and head away from the main streets."

Though the fire was across town, the flames and smoke were visible, with some smoke even blowing near the church parking lot. Ned and Jazz drove away quickly. Gabriel yelled for his wife inside the church. Maude jumped into the rental car with Copper. "Gabriel, are you going to be okay?" Liam asked as he climbed into the car.

"Yes, we'll head over to Virginia's near your parents. Thanks! Stay safe!" he responded.

"Okay, Pop and Gram should be home by now," Liam commented to Maude with a quiet urgency in his voice. He picked up his phone.

"What about the store?" Maude asked, frightened.

"The clerk's office is at the opposite end of town. It'll be okay."

"Mom! Are you guys home?" Liam yelled into the phone. "Thank God. Okay, stay put. We're headed home now." He hung up the phone and leaned his head back against the headrest. Police were putting cones up to block the roads by the church, so Liam slammed the pedal, giving them whiplash. “Sorry, kid,” he said to Maude.

“Heading to the Lincoln residence,” Liam said to the young police officer nearing the car. “I’m their son, Liam. They live on Spruce Street.” The police officer nodded.

“Okay, go straight there. The streets are closing. Go up Wright and cut across Veston. That’ll keep you far away from the flames.” The officer pointed to the hill that ran parallel to the Bible Church. Please, go quickly,” the officer stated.

Chapter Six

Before she knew it, Maude and Liam were pulling into the driveway at her grandparents' house, and both ran inside with Copper ahead of them. "Mom! Dad! Where are you?!" Liam shouted as he neared the front door.

"Hi, son," Pop answered. He walked into the kitchen where Gram was already seated. "Just listening to the scanner about the fire. How terrible. I sent everyone home and closed up for the day. Store should be out of harm's way but not safe to keep people at work," Pop explained.

"No smoke here that I can smell or see. They're closing the roads anyway. Thank God you guys are home!" Liam pulled his dad in for a hug. Gram smiled and squeezed Maude. "Any word on what caused it?" Liam asked.

"Sounds like old wiring. Marc said something about it on the scanner," Pop replied. "Help arrived quickly, though, so let's pray it's all handled and no one gets injured," he continued.

"Ned was headed over there. I'll look him up later. They'll get it under control." Liam patted his dad on the back and walked over to the refrigerator. The light popped on inside the refrigerator, and he pulled out a bottle of water and handed one to Maude too.

Gram got up and lifted her apron off the back of the basement door, just by the refrigerator. "What did you guys do today?" she asked, changing the subject.

"We got together with Ned and then, well, just did some father-daughter bonding," Liam said, winking at Maude as he chuckled and gave her an air fist-bump.

"Oh," Gram said, walking over to the desk. "We have a message I didn't notice." She pressed the button on the answering machine.

"Marguerite. This is Tom down at the Emporium. I need you to give me a call down at the Emporium. Today, if possible. Thanks." Everyone looked at the answering machine, confused.

"Arrived today, at 10:35 a.m.," the woman's automated voice finished off the message. Gram hit a button to stop the tape.

"Tom?" Marguerite asked, looking perplexed.

Maude realized this was the man whose store she was in yesterday. Maybe he was looking for her. "I was briefly in there yesterday. Maybe he is looking for me," she said.

"Must be. Weird that he'd be calling here, though. Hardly know the guy. He keeps to himself. Why were you in there, Maude? And does he even have a family, Philly?" Marguerite asked her husband.

"His family left him the store. Otherwise, no family that I know of," Pop commented. "Maude, why don't you give him a call? I can't imagine why he'd be looking for Gram," he continued.

"Me, either, but will do. Did you see the rocking chair in my room? I picked it up at the Emporium yesterday." She paused. "Do you want me to call him right now?" Maude asked.

"In a bit is fine. I didn't even know you had a new chair. The Emporium is near the Clerk's Office, so he was probably evacuated and isn't even there right now," Liam chimed in.

Much, much later that day the fire was finally under control and the smell of smoke slowly faded away. Everyone felt a new appreciation for fresh air when the scent of fresh cut grass wafted around town. Unfortunately, it took tragedy to appreciate things sometimes. Thomas Hamden had died.

Hamden's Emporium was two buildings over from the Clerk's Office. Maude didn't know where the Clerk's Office was located so she was unaware of its proximity to the Emporium. The Clerk's Office caught fire due to an overloaded power outlet. Since it was lunchtime and no one was there, the blaze took off quickly, catching a nearby curtain, then the wooden desks, and could not be stopped in time. The building next door also burnt to the ground, although fortunately it was vacant, having recently been gutted.

At the Emporium, Thomas's body was found in the office, laying on the floor. The fire was almost under control when it began to take out the Emporium. Thomas's office was on the opposite side of the store, and though the fire hadn't reached that side, he was found unresponsive. While the building was not salvageable, the good news was that Thomas passed due to a heart attack, not from lack of oxygen, and suffered no burns. His death was quick and painless. Devastating as the day had become, it was some sort of comfort to know the old man hadn't died suffering and perhaps didn't even get to see the fire consume his business.

Pop, Gram, Liam, and Maude made their way to Ardendale Central Park, which was literally in the center of town. The town gathered that evening at 7:00 p.m. to hold a candlelight vigil to honor Mr. Hamden. When Gabriel arrived, Maude realized his office was across the street. "Did Reverend Titus have any issues due to the fire?" she asked her father.

Liam looked at her with a funny look on his face. She realized Pop and Gram didn't know she knew where his office was, let alone that she'd been there after finding the first coins. "I guess in a small town like this you come to know where things are located," he covered the slip. "His place is fine, and thankfully, the other places are all also okay other than the three immediately impacted by the fire," Liam said sadly. "Boy, life is short." He shook his head and grabbed his mom with one arm, pulling her in for a hug.

Pop and Gram were both crying. They did not really know Mr. Hamden well, but sadness crippled the community. People brought flowers, notes, and balloons. Candlelight penetrated the area, and sad music played over the loudspeakers on either side of the gazebo. Many cried, others had somber looks on their faces, and others talked through tears. A woman nearby was telling her friend about the time Tommy helped her find some last-minute gifts for her sister for her birthday.

"It's so sad he had no family. His parents had long since passed, and with no uncles, aunts, cousins, or children of his own, he was alone. How sad," one woman said.

"When you said he had no family that you knew of, I guess I thought he may have been married at one point in time. He didn't even have a wife?" Maude asked Pop and Gram.

"No, honey. He took over the store from his parents. When I moved here, he was already working at the store, and his parents passed a few years after I got here. I can't remember their names, but I know he was their only child, and he didn't have any other family. He spent his life just working at the store . . ." Pop's voice trailed off as he was overcome with tears.

Maude wanted to say how sweet he was to her when she visited the other day. She wanted to say how she now understood why he was so angry that he would have lost his store to

"Big Business" as the homemade sign read. But with the tears streaming down most everyone's cheeks, hers included, she kept silent and closed her eyes to pray for peace.

Sleep that night did not come easy. Maude kept replaying her brief visit with Mr. Hamden over in her head. She remembered wanting to console him in his sadness that day. Somehow, it was an honor to get to meet him before tragedy struck. However, one of the last or perhaps the last phone call he made was to her grandparents' house. She had such a funny feeling about it, a churning in her stomach she couldn't identify as bad or good, but she just sensed *something*. When she allowed herself to realize they'd probably never know why he called, her heart ached. She found herself thinking about her mom.

After laying there for a while, she got up and walked out to the shelf of pictures and pulled one of her mom down. Hazel was standing in front of a tree with an autumn-colored scarf on. Her coat was white with black buttons; she had black polyester pants on and bushy brown hair. Her smile was infectious. Liam said her smile could light up a room, and it certainly did in this photo.

Maude stood there staring at the photo and started to cry. In her heart, she spoke to her mom, searching for *what*, she did not know.

The guest bedroom door was open a few inches across the hall. She stepped out and through the doorway, she saw her dad's rising and falling stomach moving the blankets. Though she thought of waking him, she really didn't need to talk, just felt uneasy, and wasn't exactly sure why. In this moment of sadness and uncertainty, she felt a twinge of extra gratitude for her dad. As much as he worked, and though they weren't necessarily affectionate huggers, she always, *always* felt safe talking to her dad. This visit to his parents had proven to be an affectionate one. Knowing she would be staying here, it felt different for both of them. In fact, her dad was a bit more affectionate than usual.

She grabbed a bottle of water and went back to her room but sat in her new rocking chair instead of going right to bed. She thought of Mr. Hamden and was thankful she had had the opportunity to meet such a lovely man. The conversation with him played over in her head.

Rocking gently back and forth and running her hands across the thick, long handles, the chair did not make a sound, which was surprising given the fact it was so old. Tommy had told her it was there when he inherited the store. Actually, it was in excellent condition. She knew nothing about furniture but given it was made of wood, it would have been easy to see if the wood was broken or in bad shape. She ran her hands over the smooth and even still slightly shiny arm rests. The wood was very light tan, and the back had ten wooden rungs that came above Maude's head, stacked close together, leaving no gaps. Maude stretched her arms down to the sides and grabbed the wood attaching the front to the back and ran her fingers along the inside.

Reaching for her water on the stand nearby, she sipped and prayed silently for Mr. Hamden, imagining him in heaven. Often, she thought of her mom in heaven. Her view of heaven was probably like others'—pearly gates, streets of gold, fluffy clouds, mansions, and so much light.

As she was about to stand up to go back to bed to hopefully drift off to sleep, she was surprised to feel a sort of square area on the chair that seemed like it was out of place. She ran her hands along it and couldn't help but get off the chair to take a closer look. Brushing the touch lamp to lighten the room just a tad, she kneeled to brush her hand on the area and saw a square inch area etched with a painted-over screw keeping it in place. "Just the way it was made," Maude was surprised to hear herself say out loud. *Maybe the screw needs tightening,* she thought.

She shook off the questions and went back to bed. Nevertheless, her dreams brought her back to the weird square. When she awoke again, this time at 5:00 a.m., she tiptoed to the pantry to get the toolbox. No one was awake yet, so she grabbed it and closed herself in her bedroom with it. She kneeled and undid the screw. It was on the unfinished side so when you're looking at the chair, it wouldn't be visible to anyone unless you knelt and looked underneath the chair. It was not rusted, though the paint chipped as she grunted with effort while untwisting the screw.

The clunk of the wooden piece suddenly falling off onto the floor startled her, and she was sure it woke the house. "Geez," she whispered. She didn't move, expecting to hear someone get up, but after hearing nothing, she got down horizontally to look at the space, expecting to see a simple chair's construction. Directing a flashlight toward the space, she peered in. She was astonished to see a small piece of paper folded up inside the square gap. It was shoved way to the top and free from any wear or tear. She snatched the paper and very carefully opened it. It was handwritten.

The handwriting was squiggly and not easy to make out, but the cursive letters with big bubbles for the Es and Gs were easy to read. This paper made no sense to her, but the fact it was hidden inside a rocking chair told her it must be important.

Her gut told her to wake her dad. But, as weird as this was, she knew it was nothing that couldn't wait until he was up for the day. She read and reread the paper, hoping the next read would mean something to her. But it never made sense. Despite the awkward night she had, she laid back down to sleep after putting the paper back inside the chair, lightly put the screw in, and fell asleep almost instantly.

Through restless sleep she tossed and turned, but a car horn from somewhere . . . real life or maybe a dream . . . brought her voyage from sleep to reality. A glance at her nightstand showed her the time was 10:00 a.m. "Whoa! Holy cow," she shouted and jumped up, shocked that she'd slept so late. In her sleepy haze, she struggled to make sense of the previous night. She remembered the paper and squatted down next to the rocking chair to see if it had been a dream. Tapping around for the square and feeling that the odd area was indeed there and loose just as she'd left it, she stood, sighed, relaxed her shoulders, and resolved to stay calm.

"I have to get ready," Maude said to herself and walked to the restroom to shower and dress. She turned on her audio Bible devotional to listen as she tipped her head upside down to put her hair in a ponytail, put on a little eyeliner and pink eye shadow, and rubbed on some lip gloss as she walked down the hallway.

Pop and Gram had gone to work, and Dad was sitting in the living room on the dark brown recliner sipping coffee, watching Sports Center. "Hi, honey," he said to her without turning around. "Did you sleep well?" he asked her, smiling at her with his sleepy face.

"Not much. I was restless and did some investigating," Maude told him.

"Oh?" He leaned over to sip his coffee as he looked at her out of the corner of his eye. "What about?" he asked.

"Okay, so this is all out-of-this-world stuff, but the weirdest thing happened." She tried to keep her face neutral. "Remember when I told you I picked up a rocking chair from Hamden's Emporium?" Liam nodded and Maude sat down in the other recliner. "Well, he told me that he didn't know much about it, that it was there when he inherited the store, and it had been in the front window. I mean it appears to be in excellent condition, like maybe it was never sat in and was only used as a window display." Liam looked at her but said nothing. "Well, I couldn't sleep last night so I sat down to rock and relax but found something super bizarre." His eyebrows went up. "There is basically a small square portion on the bottom side of the rocking chair that I opened up. Inside was a piece of paper with names and dates on it," she blurted out, and then held her breath.

"What?" His eyes widened. "Let me see." He sat up, and Maude led him to the chair. She got out the screwdriver and handed it to her dad. Pointing to where the area was, her dad knelt and undid the screw, and pulled the paper out. He read it without speaking a word. It was silent for a long while, and finally he said, "I have absolutely no idea." He read and reread the paper, just as she'd done.

He kept the paper folded in his hand but headed back to the recliner. "I'll take a photo with my phone." The lonesome paper looked so tiny and out of place on the recliner. Liam snapped photos from a few angles, some close and some from a distance. "Maudie, I know this is super bizarre. No doubt, kiddo. But I think it really doesn't matter what this is. I vaguely remember this chair sitting in that store. It's probably the same one, and you're right that it sat in the front window. I mean, if it's been there all these years, I don't think it means anything *for us*." He read the paper again. "I'm just going to put it back together," he said, while folding the paper back up into the same creased lines and then put it back into its crevice. He put the square back into place and stood up. "Weird, but not sure what to do about it," was Liam's final comment.

He took the toolbox, which was still sitting on the bedroom floor, and brought it back to the pantry. Maude sat back down in the living room, shrugged her shoulders, and tried to convince herself this was nothing.

Liam's words interrupted her thoughts. "Changing the

subject here, Maudie, planned to have lunch with Ned and his wife and kids today. I'd like you to come. Pop and Gram will be out and about for a while, so we can stop by the shop and then have lunch," he said.

Maude nodded. "Good to catch up while you're in town," she said, disappointed he seemed so nonchalant about the paper in the rocking chair. She thought about his words—he remembered the chair sitting there, and if the paper had been in there for that many years, indeed it probably wasn't significant for them. *Maybe people just react differently to things,* she thought to herself. She decided that she'd go out and enjoy the day with her dad and try not to think about the mysterious paper.

"Yep! So, let's get ready to head out," Liam said as he walked down the hall to the guest room to change. Maude shook the hidden rocking chair note out of her head and went to grab her purse.

Chapter Seven

The Square Meal Diner was located just two blocks from the horrible fire that ripped apart the Clerk's Office, the vacant building next to it, and part of Hamden's Emporium. It was on the west end of town, down the road from some smaller Mom-and-Pop shops. The building where the diner had been was relatively small, but the inside space had plenty of room for twenty booths, ten tables, and a bar area, though the place served no alcohol. The building was light brown with red shutters and a red matching roof. It almost appeared to be a house and frankly, if the sign on the side and top of the building didn't say, "The Square Meal Diner," people might not have known it was a diner.

Inside, the walls were adorned with inspirational quotes printed in large type and sporadically placed around the rooms against a background of white wallpaper with a light purple border. Maya Angelou, Wayne Dyer, Joel Osteen, and Eleanor Roosevelt were the first ones visible as someone walked in the door—a door made of big see-through glass with a heavy, metal frame.

The Morgans, who owned the diner, were wonderful people. Lucy went above and beyond to make the place look welcoming and decorated for each holiday and season. Ned was "Mr. Fix It" and kept everything in working order. Lucy greeted Liam and Maude at the door. She was wearing a simple white, knee-length, one-piece uniform with a blue apron. "The Square Meal Diner" was printed on her apron in simple bold pink letters.

"Oh my gosh, Liam! Hello! And Maude? Wow! You are just beautiful," Lucy exclaimed as they all walked in the door. She hugged Liam and then Maude. "How wonderful to see you both!" She grabbed menus and led them to a booth halfway down the length of the diner. "Coffee, Liam?" He nodded. "Maude? What would you like?" she asked.

"Orange juice, please," Maude replied.

"You got it!" she enthusiastically replied. "Ned will be right out." She headed behind the bar to pour coffee into a carafe. Maude watched as Lucy grabbed a clear glass cup and hit the button on the juice machine. She reached under the counter for something while the juice poured out on its own. It clicked off when the glass was nearly full. She placed the orange juice, table settings, carafe of coffee, two upside down coffee cups, plus a bowl of creamers on a tray, and headed over to the booth. "Liam, how's business?" she asked. The glassware clanked as she placed it on the table.

"Busy as ever! Lucy, this place is looking great! Ned said business has been good?" Liam asked.

"Yes! Like or dislike the Schneider Construction company, they are great patrons here, and we keep busy with the regulars, and of course, out-of-towners too. Can't complain! We're blessed."

Lucy's eyes suddenly sparkled. "Maude, I hear you're training to take over your grandparents' bookstore. Great place! They've done a remarkable job with it. It's always busy, and it looks great." She patted Maude's wrist as she spoke.

"Yes. I'm excited!" Maude said. Her own words surprised her. She knew she enjoyed working there, even enjoyed learning the ropes so she could take over. But suddenly, she was genuinely excited to make the store hers someday. *Wow*. All the pieces were falling into place for her to stay in Ardendale. She surprised herself with the emotion this thought brought on.

Her dad's chatter with Lucy interrupted her thoughts. When she looked over at her dad and saw him smiling at her, she felt a twinge of sadness, knowing she'd be without him and their life outside of Ardendale. Yet she didn't feel frightened, just sad—typical for this situation, she guessed.

"Well, this town is going to grow. Having young blood here to continue a tradition like your grandparents' store? Incredible!" Lucy added. She looked up to the ceiling and mouthed, "Thank you," to God.

Before Maude could respond, a half door that led from the backroom to the dining area swung open, alerting them that Ned was coming. He placed a hand on the small of his wife's back, kissed her forehead, and sat down next to Liam. He grabbed the spare cup and poured himself coffee from the carafe.

"Be back in a few," Lucy said, winking.

"Hey, guys! How's things today?" Ned asked. He shook hands with Liam and fist-bumped Maude.

"I have to head over to Tommy's house after this. Such sadness. What a good man he was." Ned's eyes drifted off to the distance.

"His house? Why, Mr. Morgan?" Maude asked.

"Oh, sweetie. Tommy didn't have any family—no children, no siblings, and his parents passed ages ago. When someone does not designate someone to their estate, there is no one to go through their belongings or to clean out the house or do pertinent paperwork. In a case like this, normally the state would appoint an executor to oversee dispersal, but since he was a regular parishioner of the church, the church is allowed to help. I'm a deacon and therefore, I'll go over with another deacon and with Gabriel to sift through things. We do know there is a will though. Marian McCarthy is on that right now," Ned replied.

"Gotcha. Well, that is sad he didn't have a family," Maude said.

"True, but he was a kind, good man—everyone knew him. He mostly kept to himself but always showed kindness and occasionally, he even visited here. We had him over for Thanksgiving dinner once. The other years he insisted he was fine by himself. But one year, he came. He didn't talk much, but he was a wholesome, good business man," Ned said, softly.

"Good you're able to help. I'm glad to help if I can do anything," Liam said, sipping his coffee after pouring in just one little packet of creamer.

"Actually, we may need help with furniture in a few days. I assume it'll be donated, unless his will says otherwise. We'll have to move everything out for the church to come clean up before the house can be sold. This will most likely be next week. You were headed back tomorrow?" Ned asked.

"Actually, the next day. I can push back a few meetings to extend my stay, but I have to be back next week. Is there anything I can do in the meantime?" Liam asked.

"Not sure. This is the first I've had to do this. It's happened before, but we were out of town on a family vacation last time, so I wasn't around to help. I'll see what you can do, if anything," Ned replied.

Just then, Maude noticed an old couple walking by. She recognized them as Bernie and Shirley, from The Books Are Here. Coincidentally, Lucy sat them right next to their booth. "How are you feeling, Bern? Heard you were a little under the weather the other day," Maude overheard Lucy ask them.

"Just low blood sugar. They checked things over and off I

went. Shirley is keeping an eye on me now." Maude saw Shirley smile and was sure Bernie must have winked at her.

"Yep. Thanks to the help of a sweet girl who works there, it was quick work, and we got him taken care of." Shirley was facing Maude's direction and recognized her. Suddenly, her eyes lit up and she lifted her arm to point in Maude's direction. "This here is the girl who helped my Bernie! Sweetie?" Shirley stood up.

Maude stood and went over to their table. Shirley put her right hand on Maude's left arm and rubbed it. "Thank you again for getting help for Bernie." Shirley smiled looking from Maude to Bernie.

Maude nodded. "Happy to help, ma'am. Glad you're feeling better," Maude commented. She looked at Bernie. There was an awkward silence. Maude was not big on being the center of attention, so she didn't know what else to say. She felt relieved he was better, and even proud of herself for her quick thinking the morning of the incident, but she felt silly saying those things. "Anyone would have called for help. I am just glad I happened to be there at the right time," she said and winked, as if that would help alleviate how awkward she felt.

"Marc, buddy, how are ya?" Ned's voice interrupted her thoughts. She glanced over to see Marc, the EMT she had been attracted to, standing at her table. She felt her cheeks flush and drew a complete blank as to what to say.

"Good! Thanks!" Marc nodded in Liam's direction and stepped behind Maude and kissed Shirley on the cheek, squeezing her shoulder, giving her a half hug. He noticed Maude and smiled. He walked back behind her and slipped into the booth next to Bernie. "Hi, Pops!" He put his arm on Bernie's shoulders and gave him a squeeze. "Glad you're feeling better. "Do you need anything?"

Maude still stood there, feeling more awkward than before.

"Good to see you," she whispered. She half waved and quickly slipped back into her booth. She made a conscious effort to calm her heart and turned her blushing face down. She looked at Marc's head and felt that butterfly feeling she had originally felt the first time she saw him. Desperate to get rid of her blushing cheeks, she focused on Ned and her dad's conversation. Then she heard a familiar voice and spun around to look. It was Gabriel headed for their booth.

"Hi, everyone," Gabriel chimed. Marc came over to their table at the same time. "Hey!" Gabriel said excitedly to Marc. "Liam, I know you know this, but I guess Maude wouldn't know. This is my grandson, Marc," Gabriel said. Maude was sure her jaw dropped. She had no idea Gabriel and Marc were related, let alone grandfather and grandson. This was the first trip to Ardendale during which she had met either one of them, but she had at least *heard* of Gabriel before. It occurred to her she never gave much thought to what family he may have.

Maude looked up at both of them. "Nice to meet you," she managed to get out.

"Again," Marc replied with a smile. Maude didn't say anything, embarrassed. "We met briefly the other day. She called us for help with Bernie."

Just then, Lucy walked back to the table. "Oh, that was you, honey?" Lucy asked.

Maude nodded. "I just called the ambulance when I came across Bernie not feeling well." She was matter of fact. If she had any question how tight knit this community was after the candlelight vigil for Mr. Hamden, she no longer questioned it. A simple call for help for someone in need meant the town thought she was some sort of hero. "Any good and decent person would have done the same thing," she stated.

"I haven't seen you since you were tiny," Liam said with a chuckle.

Gabriel sat next to Ned and swallowed a sip of the coffee Lucy had placed in front of him. "Yes. I guess the last time you would have seen him was that long ago. Wow." Gabriel paused. "He is Adelaide's son, that's for sure. He takes after her." Marc smiled in Liam's direction and the two shook hands.

"Good to meet you, er, again," Liam commented.

"You, too, sir. I won't interrupt, just wondering what time you wanted me to set up for Vacation Bible School, Grandpa?" Marc asked Gabriel.

"Two is fine. You'll be primarily in my office and the back loft. But can you help set up the sanctuary too?" Gabriel asked Marc, then turned to look at everyone else. "My grandson here is running the youth group for the church. Vacation Bible School starts Monday, and he is going to be teaching the junior high kids. We usually just do the program for kids under twelve, but we wanted to expand this year to see if there was interest," Gabriel told the table.

"Wow, Marc! EMT and heavily involved in Grandpa's church? You sound just like your grandpa. Busy!" Liam smiled.

"Yes, lots going on, but it's how I grew up. Wouldn't have it any other way," Marc told Liam, while patting his grandpa Gabriel on the back.

"Where is Adelaide and Earl?" Liam asked Gabriel. "Still teaching?"

Gabriel nodded his head. Marc chimed in. "Mom and Dad are teaching here at the elementary school."

Lucy walked over just then with a notepad. Marc and Gabriel said goodbye and headed over to the bar, and Liam, Ned, and Maude placed their orders. They chatted some more after ordering, and when finished with their meals, headed out. Maude and Liam drove over to the bookstore, while Ned went over to Mr. Hamden's place. On the way to the bookstore, Liam complimented Maude on calling the ambulance for help with Bernie.

"Honestly, Dad, it was no big deal. I just saw he needed help and called," she responded.

"Maudie, when you're in a small town like this, the littlest of deeds do not go unnoticed. Diabetes is nothing to mess around with, and you helped someone who really needed it, plain and simple. Accept the compliments." He smiled at her and patted her knee.

Maude shrugged her shoulders. "Thanks. People show real southern hospitality, and we're not even in the South." She laughed at her own joke.

"True. I loved growing up here. Don't get me wrong though —there can be gossip and small-town *stuff* that comes with it, but as you get older, that stuff just rolls off. The majority of people here are real and genuine, and they're just living their lives, going for coffee, stopping at the post office, greeting people on the way, planting in their gardens, meeting friends for lunch, going to the supermarket for groceries, making dinner on the grill, and discussing their families with the neighbors. It's a great place to live, and it was rewarding to grow up here," Liam responded. "It instilled good value in me and a work ethic that has served me well."

With that, Ned changed the topic of discussion to business at the bookstore. And they continued the discussion as they went over to the store.

At The Books Are Here, it was business as usual. Liam sat in the back office with Maude and his parents. Marian McCarthy, the main lawyer in town, joined them. Her attendance came as a surprise to Maude, but it didn't seem to surprise anyone else. In fact, Liam even had an extra cup of coffee prepared upon her arrival. Clearly, they all knew she was coming.

"Hi, Maude. I am happy to meet you. Your family are all wonderful people. You come from good genes!" Marian said kindly as she looked over at Marguerite and winked.

Gram smiled back and pulled out a chair to sit down. Pop was already seated, and Liam was on the other side of Marian. "Your grandparents wanted to go over some paperwork with you," Marian said, talking to Maude. "They want to get some papers signed to guarantee the future of this business." Marian glanced over at Pop and Gram. "Let me be clear. We understand it is too soon to give you *everything*. After all, you are deciding on your future. However, your grandparents have asked that I draw up the papers to sign the store over to your dad—unless you're ready to accept full ownership right now, Maude. This is the reason I am here today," she finished, opening the file.

Liam looked at Maude. "I am accepting responsibility for the store. Mom and Dad will continue to run things, training you to take over. But for now, the paperwork will legally make it mine. I will give it all over to you—if and when you are ready," he stated, his eyes full of compassion.

"Okay. Makes sense," Maude responded. Internally, she was surprised at the rapid speed this was all taking place. She hadn't been in town for long enough to train to take over ownership, and here her grandparents were giving up control. She felt worried and suddenly blurted out, "Pop and Gram, is everything okay, health-wise? And what if a big decision needs to be made and Dad isn't here?"

"Oh, honey. We're fine! Thanks be to God," Gram responded, even giggling a little.

"This paperwork gives your dad legal responsibility, but it is contingent on if your grandparents become, God forbid, of unsound mind. They are still legally *allowed* to run things, just as they do right now. This will simply cover them in case of—emergency," Marian paused, choosing her words carefully.

"Pop and Gram are fine, Maudie." Liam squeezed Maude's hand. "Thank God!" He looked over at Pop and Gram.

"Thank God, indeed!" Marian said, smiling.

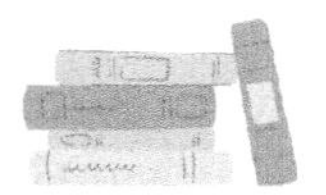

Once they signed the papers, Maude and Liam spent a few hours at the store going over documents pertaining to ordering, hiring, employee rights, and many, *many* other forms. When they left to head back to Pop and Gram's house, Maude and Liam had a brief chat. "It's a lot to take in, honey. The number one thing I want you to remember is that no one is pressuring you. If you decide living here, running the store, taking things over is not for you, then no harm done." When Maude didn't respond, he continued, "Pop and Gram just want to be sure their I's are dotted and their T's are crossed. That's all. *Don't worry.* Take your time. *But* . . . don't lead them astray," he continued. Liam shook his head. "I know you won't hurt them. I just mean if you're feeling this just absolutely isn't for you, be honest and up front about it." He paused. "This is all very big stuff. No one would blame you for bailing."

"I can't answer everything right now. But I really like working at the store. I *do* want to do it. But I'm not ready to sign any papers—not yet. But Dad, what if, God forbid, something happens to Pop and Gram and it's not signed to me?" Maude asked her dad.

"It's not something I want to think about. But if anything were to happen, I could take a leave to come to town to figure things out." There was a long pause. "Things will all fall into place," he said, nodding at his own words.

They pulled up to the house. Liam parked out front so Pop and Gram could park in the driveway. They had followed each other home. Liam's cell rang as he shut the engine off. "It's Ned," he said to Maude. "Hey, buddy." Maude could barely make out Ned's voice coming through the phone. She hopped out of the car and walked into the house. Gram was hanging her purse on the coat rack, and Pop threw his keys on the counter. "Everything okay, honey?" Gram asked Maude.

"Yes, Gram," Maude reassured her. She wanted to say she felt good about staying here to run the store and that her dad could help if anything happened. But it was too difficult to think about anything morbid, so she decided to not say what was on her mind. Clearly, Pop and Gram were in good shape, thanks be to God. They had a good, long many years ahead. At the thought, she felt a twinge of delight in her stomach.

Pop yawned. "My lovies, I think I'm going to go take a nap." He looked around. "Where is your dad?"

"Ned called. He's just in the car talking," Maude replied. Maude looked over at Gram. "Gram, let's sit on the screened porch?" she asked. She was feeling close to her grandparents after the morbid thoughts that had haunted the last few hours.

Maude and Marguerite shared some common hobbies, some of life's simple pleasures. They enjoyed watching *The Young and the Restless* together and drinking hot tea. Both were simple pastimes made extra special when enjoyed in each other's company. When Maude was not in Ardendale, she watched *The Young and the Restless* religiously, always thinking of Gram, even talking out loud to the TV at times. She knew Gram was thinking of her in those times too. Pop and Gram were not much for texting or social media, but they did know how to email, and she and Gram emailed about the show from time to time. Since the show had already aired for the day, they decided to share their time together on the porch with hot tea.

Maude forgot that her dad was on the phone. As she and

Gram carried their cups to the screened-in porch attached to Maude's room, her phone chimed, signifying a text. She put her tea down on the built-in cup holder in between the two seats. She lifted the phone out of her pocket and unlocked the screen with a swipe. She read a text from her dad. "Ned needs help with some things. Let Pop and Gram know I'll be back later. Love you all." Maude read the text aloud to Gram. Since Pop was sleeping and nothing was really going on at the house, Maude was glad her dad went off to help Ned with whatever he needed.

"So, honey. What's up?" Gram smiled at Maude. Maude felt intense love as she looked at Gram with her light blue eyes and curly, white hair. Gram thought of herself as spunky and saying, "What's up?" was her version of *being hip*.

Maude laughed out loud just thinking about it. "Oh, Gram, I love you." They both smiled.

Copper walked onto the porch. "Hi, Copper!" Maude said. The dog walked in a small circle and curled up on the ground exactly in between the two women. Gram reached down to rub Copper's back.

"Copper has been with us for ten years. She came from a family of purebreds." Gram reached down to pet her again. "Before her, we had her mom. My parents had purebred Dobermans also," Gram told Maude.

Just then, the doorbell rang. Gram and Maude silently gave each other a look of frustration at the interruption. "I got it," Maude said as she stood up and made her way to the front door in the kitchen. She opened the door to see Mr. and Mrs. Mason, her grandparents' neighbors, smiling at her. "Hello, Mr. and Mrs. Mason!" Maude said, truly glad to see them.

"Maude! Hello, honey!" Mrs. Mason said while reaching in for a hug. "Please, you can call us Joann and Stanley," she said, motioning between she and her husband. "Your grandparents said you were coming to stay. We wanted to welcome you sooner, but we were visiting our daughter. Just got home this morning. Here is some homemade soup. Enjoy!" Joann smiled, while holding out a container.

"Oh, my goodness. Thanks! Please come in!" Maude replied.

"We don't want to intrude. We just wanted to welcome you. If you ever need anything, you know where we live!" Joann winked.

"Thank you! But please, come on in. My dad is in town, though not here at the moment. I am sure he'd love to see you." Maude stepped out of the way to allow the Masons to walk in. They obliged and Gram also walked into the kitchen. They exchanged hellos. The Masons invited everyone over to their house to sit on their big back deck. Gram left a note for Pop so he would know where they were when he woke up.

They headed next door and Maude kept her cell phone in her pocket so that she could text her dad to let him know where they all were.

The visit was lovely. Mrs. Mason was always good for a motivational, inspiring talk. She was a beautiful, strong woman who also served as the school nurse. But what Maude appreciated most about her was her love and care. She remembered a time during a summer visit when she was much younger. Maude had confided in her about some peer pressure issues she'd faced that year. Though she had remained true to herself and hadn't given in, Mrs. Mason had a way of reinforcing that she was great just as she was, and if anyone thought differently, she shouldn't ever listen to them.

Liam often told Maude she had an old soul because she preferred spending time with "the old folks" as he called his generation. But Maude loved it. She enjoyed spending time with Pop and Gram and their neighbors and hearing stories of her dad and the Mason's children, about their growing up and adventures together. For Maude, it felt like home. The stories never got old. The warmth the neighbors showed and the reassurance Mrs. Mason gave was more special to Maude than she could express.

Chapter Eight

As the day went on, Maude hadn't heard from her dad, despite the text she sent to let him know they were at the neighbor's house. Since Ned was cleaning out Mr. Hamden's house, she figured it must be an emotional task and her dad was, no doubt, trying to offer his support. So, she wasn't surprised when Liam pulled up at dusk. She and her grandparents had long since left the Masons and were comfy at home.

Her grandparents were in their pajamas, nearly asleep. Pop was watching a baseball game in the living room, occasionally snoring in his recliner with his feet up. Gram was doing a crossword puzzle though she rested her head on her palm and dozed off from time to time. Maude was on the ugly couch reading and Copper was fast asleep. Finally, Liam walked in, looking exhausted. His eyes were dark, with bags under them. The sparkle in his eye was gone. He waved unenthusiastically. "Sorry to be so late. We'll catch up in the morning." Liam attempted a smile at Maude.

"Okay," Maude said, feeling bad about what an emotional

day it must have been. Pop and Gram slept right through the ten-second conversation. She decided to head to bed herself.

Maude had forgotten about the hidden note in the rocking chair until she dreamt about it that night. In her dream, Mr. Hamden was sweeping the Emporium, and Maude was watching him. He didn't see her, and somehow, she knew that she was invisible in the dream, not actually a customer in the store. Mr. Hamden leaned the broom against the front counter and picked up a small sheet of paper. He rubbed the paper between his fingers as he walked over to the rocking chair in the front window. The square portion was already undone and sitting on the seat. Tommy reached the note up into the crevice and squatted down to re-screw the area back in. When he stood up, he mumbled something Maude couldn't understand. Though she wasn't physically in the store, and it seemed Tommy wasn't aware of her presence, he suddenly looked her directly in the eyes.

"The clue is in my will," he said.

Before Maude could respond, the room pulled away from grasp, as though Maude were on roller skates and someone was pulling her. As the store completely faded from sight, she began to feel like she was falling. She jerked herself awake, sweaty under the sheets.

She looked over at the rocking chair. It hadn't moved, and while she realized it was just a dream, she felt spooked. She sat up in bed and replayed Mr. Hamden's words to her, over and over, and tried to find something else in the dream to bring some sort of answer. Flicking on the side night lamp, she remembered thinking about Mr. Hamden's house, possessions, and will before falling asleep. It made sense she dreamt about him. But "the clue is in my will" was freaky and did not sit well, even after she got up. She prayed for wisdom and peace, then flicked her radio on, curling back up in bed. She tossed and turned, her stomach in a knot. All she could do was pray.

Dear Lord, please give me peace. Forgive me for my wrongs. Right now, I need strength, peace, and wisdom. I feel frightened and spooked, and other than the nightmare, I have no reason to feel that way. Help my dad as he must be drained after helping Ned yesterday. Keep my grandparents healthy and help me to learn the ropes at the store. I am feeling more and more like I belong here. Thank you for that. In Jesus' name I pray, Amen.

Maude ended the prayer feeling a little better. It wasn't long after that she finally fell back asleep. She had no more dreams and when she woke up, the first thing she thought of was her dad, not the haunting, rocking chair dream.

In the morning, she hopped in the shower then came back to get dressed in her room. She was dressed but still applying her makeup when there was a light knock on her door. "Maude?" It was Liam's voice. "Are you decent?" he asked her.

"Hey, Dad. Yep, come on in," Maude replied.

She was puckering her lips, making a fish face as she applied blush to her cheekbones. Liam sat down in the rocking chair, which made Maude think of the nightmare she'd had last night. She didn't want to think about it, so she smiled over at her dad. It was the first time she'd seen his face since he walked into the house looking exhausted last night. He looked far worse now. His eyes were wrinkled, his hair disarrayed, and he was wearing the same clothes from last night.

"Maudie. I need to talk to you," he suddenly said. The way he looked was like nothing Maude had ever seen, and his words just sat in the air. Maude felt afraid. Her dad was the consummate professional in his career. He was always well put together. She didn't remember a lot about the times when her mom died, but she assumed this was how he must have appeared. Suddenly, she thought about Pop and Gram.

"Oh my gosh, are Pop and Gram alright?" she half-shouted.

He looked her in the eyes. "Yes, sweetie, they are fine. This isn't about them . . . well *it is* . . . but it's more about us as a family." Liam sat down in the rocking chair and crossed his legs. Maude sat down on the far side of the bed away from the chair, almost feeling like she needed to not be close in proximity to her dad, as though physical distance could cushion the blow she was probably about to receive. The way her dad appeared and was acting was foreign to her. Her skin felt clammy, and her mind wandered to what could be going on. *Did I do something wrong?* She thought.

Distracting herself, she thought of all the times her dad said to her, "Maude, you're going to make mistakes and mess up sometimes. We *all* do. The first thing to know is that you are no better than anyone else, but at the same time, no one is better than you. Whatever you do, seek forgiveness, and as long as you can look at yourself in the mirror in the morning, it'll be okay. Do your best. You're a good kid. I trust you to make good choices. Don't leave a trail of mistakes behind you." Maude's memory of that conversation she'd heard so many times temporarily removed her from the thick air in the room.

"Dad, did I do something wrong?" Maude prayed in her head for guidance.

"I don't know. Did you?" He slyly giggled. It definitely lightened the mood. Maude smiled back.

"Okay, so what is it?" she asked him, her makeup half done and pajamas strewn on the bed next to where she sat.

"Maudie. I went over to Tommy Hamden's house yesterday. Ned called me and said that there was an urgent matter he needed my help with. I don't know what I expected, but it wasn't this." He looked down. "There was a will. Fortunately, Tommy had made plans. It is a legal document with copies for all parties, and well, there was one for our family." He glanced up to make eye contact with Maude.

"*Our* family? I'm confused," Maude said.

"Okay, so this is a long and complicated story. I had to hear it, read it, and study it repeatedly. I still don't know if I truly understand all of it," he began. She saw his jaw tighten as he clenched his teeth. "Those names on that rocking chair?" It must have occurred to him that he was sitting in the rocking chair because he hopped up as if it was on fire and plopped down on the other side of the bed opposite of where Maude was sitting. "The paper inside this rocking chair . . . makes sense now," he said, leaning down to glance at the square section. Maude said nothing, aching for more information. "I'm so short on sleep that I can't even be sure of the names right now," Liam said and paused for a minute.

She sat in silence, allowing her dad to take his time. His tired eyes and demeanor made it clear he was out of sorts. Silently, she prayed for him, for the family, for their peace of mind. This seemed like a weird dream.

After a short silence, he turned on the bed to look directly at Maude. "First, I think you need to understand a few things. This town is very old. In the 1800s, the *houses* were out in the woods where Copper took off to. Then, the Civil War happened, and people started to build homes where we are *now*, which was just woods *back then*. It basically flip-flopped. So, 200 plus years later, all of that area from the 1800s is now a vacant, woodsy lot filled with wildlife. I mean you saw how it is nothing now, although the foundation was a huge surprise. Things switched," he said as he crossed his arms to show emphasis. "With most of the current town's structures built in the latter part of the 1800s, they don't live up to safety standards. Most had electricity added in the nineteenth century, but even the *newer* homes aren't necessarily up to code. Think of it like if you had a home with only a few outlets, old appliances, and weak, outdated wiring, corroding pipes, and other *things*. Many structures are simply wearing out in the weather. People do their best to keep a roof over their heads! But the fact of the matter is that houses are one thing, but businesses need to meet code requirements."

Liam stood for a moment and paced. Then, he sat back down. "I know some people—okay *most*—were angry when Schneider's came in to revitalize the town. These little Mom and Pop shops are what made Ardendale so quaint." He paused, emotional. "It goes deeper than this, though. People help each other here. The Gardeners Club helped older families to keep the town looking beautiful. Friends help paint, build decks, change wallpaper, all the things to help others. The people, this place . . . is just full of cherished memories for me." He swallowed hard. "I'm pleased with my life and career, but it is the polar opposite from here. After your mom died, I built a successful career that no one could knock down. I needed to raise you and somehow keep my head above water, so the only way I knew to do that was to work nonstop and try not to feel the grief of losing Hazel." He looked off to the distance, his lip trembling slightly. To see his lip tremble, Maude teared up.

"You did the best you could, Dad," was all she could muster.

He smiled at her. "Thanks, sweetie. This is not about me, but I guess I want to try to explain how all this happened." He stood up and looked at the rocking chair. "Well, guess this is appropriate to sit here," he said as he sat back down in the chair. He rubbed the handles with his palms and was silent for a moment. "For so many people, they felt angry about the possibility of losing their businesses. I know in most cases, Schneider Construction LLC, the company that came to Ardendale, offered to let family companies keep their management. But the reality is, *the way things used to be* would not be the same for people. So, for someone like Tom Hamden, it was devastating. He was an only child with no next of kin. So, about a year ago, he employed an old historian friend from out of town named

Lester. It is my guess that he wanted to discretely research his heritage and not allow even the most trustworthy of men, not even Gabriel, to know anything. Lester took a long time but came upon the fact that despite no immediate next of kin, he did have relatives he didn't know about. In fact, it turns out he had relatives right here in Ardendale." Liam looked directly into Maude's eyes. "*Us*," he said.

"What?!" Maude felt confused and a little nervous.

He took out a piece of paper from his back pocket. It was folded up, and though Maude couldn't see it clearly from where she was sitting, it was clear from the black streaks that it was a photocopy. Liam didn't get up to show her the paper. Instead, he looked at it and kept talking. "This paper can explain things better than I can. It turns out that in 1825, identical twin girls were born in Benston. Their names were Claire and Christine, but their parents gave them to an orphanage. Before you ask, no reason given, so who knows why? Twins cost more money, and back then, there weren't the luxuries there are today for caring for children. Whatever the reason, they were adopted by separate families and never knew about each other. Claire grew up in Ardendale, however. She was here her entire life, as were her children and her children's children. Christine, on the other hand, lived 500-plus miles away and never knew Ardendale." He paused, fiddling with the paper in his hands, studying it over to be sure he got the facts correct.

"Whoa," Maude said.

"Here. You should see this." Liam waved Maude over. She walked over and sat on the bed near to the rocking chair as her dad pulled the chair closer. He held the photocopy, which was signed at the bottom. She didn't recognize most of the names, but one was Mr. Hamden's, one was Mr. Hamden's historian friend Lester Welch, and one name she recognized as Judge Buckley, the local judge, though she'd never met him. It was notarized and dated. It was a family tree with dozens of names, separated by sides, with a few arrows. At first sight, it seemed like it'd be too difficult to understand, but as she read on, it made sense, and she was shocked to see her name, her dad's name, and her grandparents' names there toward the bottom. She looked at her dad, speechless, wanting more information.

"Tell me more. I think I'll understand more if you tell me," Maude said, her stomach in knots.

"Around 1895, a man named Samuel Hamden married Eliza Connors. Eliza died giving birth to Celestia. Samuel was devastated, absolutely distraught to lose his wife and now was left with a baby girl. He panicked. *I can relate*." Liam's voice trailed off. "I am sure he loved his daughter, but he ran away from the pain. Somehow, he ended up in Ardendale, where he took years to start a new life. He met Faith O'Brien and married her four years later, in 1899, I assume not ever telling her about his child, and maybe not about his widow, either. But we'll never know for sure." He took a deep breath, watching Maude to see if she could follow any of this. He continued, "Their son's name was Maxwell Hamden. Therefore, Celestia and Maxwell are technically half siblings. But again, they had no idea about each other." He paused again, trying to read Maude's face. "Shall I go on?" Liam asked her.

After a long pause, she replied, "Hamden? Coincidence? Yes, go on."

"No coincidence. But first, let me tell you that Celestia was raised by her grandparents, and therefore her last name was changed to their last name, Connors. Celestia married John Williams and had Grandma Marguerite."

When Maude said nothing, he continued, "This is a lot to take in. Hopefully this family tree will make things clearer for you. He handed it over to her, then continued, "Pop moved to Ardendale when he was fifteen. His parents, your great-grandparents, got teaching jobs here and settled in. He met Gram at college, though, and they fell in love and came back here and stayed. Since Gram was an only child, her parents visited here once or twice, but mostly Pop and Gram visited them because her parents' old age began to prevent too much travel."

Liam took a deep breath. "In the meantime, Maxwell Hamden married Barb Clark who opened the Emporium in 1945. That was the same year Tommy Hamden was born—their one and only child. Again, Tommy had no wife or children, so when Schneider's came in to redo his store, he was angry, disappointed, and frustrated. He decided to take his time and try to stretch it out as long as he could. It was a year before he had to start cleaning the store out. In that year, he hired Lester and had him dig in the way that ancestry and historical people do. He wanted to find out about any family he may have. In that year, his health had deteriorated, perhaps from old age or perhaps from heartbreak. He knew his days were numbered, and he wanted to leave whatever he had left, which wasn't much, to someone. He was about to lose his store, and he felt he wanted to leave some impact on someone, that his life wasn't lived in vain."

"Dad! Wait, Mr. Hamden called Gram the day of the fire!" Suddenly, Maude started to fit the pieces together.

"Yep. It appears he wanted to tell her this whole story. This paperwork is dated less than a month ago. It appears to be new knowledge." He swallowed hard. "The thing is, he left Gram everything. Granted, he was living off his bank accounts including retirement, so it doesn't appear to be much. The house he left to the church, and the store was purchased by Schneider's already. But his possessions and retirement and bank accounts—he left all of those to Gram.

He reached over to brush Maude's hair out of her face. "You okay?" he asked her.

"Yea," she said, pausing as she tried to follow the family tree in her hands. "So those names on the paper in the rocking chair, they're the same names on here. Why would they be hidden in the chair?" she said, not really expecting an answer.

"It would appear that his parents had been researching, too, but hadn't gotten very far. With the Internet now, finding information back then was not as easy as it is today. We don't have all the answers, but it appears that is the reason for the paper. He stood up and walked in a circle, stretching his back.

"Wow, so do Pop and Gram know?" Maude asked her dad.

"Not yet. I wanted to tell you first. Ned and Gabriel found the information yesterday afternoon and alerted me. We spent the rest of the day talking it out and understanding it as best we could. It made cleaning out his house more emotional," he said. "I know Gram won't want his furniture, so we can let the church use it along with the house to help the community. However, they can't legally take it away until we tell her everything and she signs it over." He inhaled deeply. "Ned and Gabriel are available to help me sit down with Pop and Gram to try to explain all this. I also called Marian McCarthy to see if she can make some sense of the legal stuff," he said.

"Well, I think we should have this conversation here, not at the store. Whatever you need from me, I'm here. It's a lot to take in, but it's not something we can't all be here to support Gram through," Maude said.

"I've already called to extend my leave for a few more days. I'll be heading back just hours before I absolutely have to be there. I want to be here to support them. And, Maude, whatever you decide to do is entirely up to you, but for now at least, I am glad you are here to stay with them, at least for a while." He put his arm around her shoulders and gave her a side squeeze.

"About that, Dad . . ." She took a deep breath and continued, "When they gave me the opportunity, I originally thought I'd give it a try because I don't do much back home. I was unsettled with college and never really felt at home there, although I admit I always did feel at home when we visited here. As the weeks have gone on, I've come to understand why you and Pop and Gram love it here so much. It is exactly the opposite of where I grew up, and there is nothing wrong with it there, not at all. In fact, millions love it there. But for me, I like the slow pace of this town. I like the people. I like the homey feel I get when I'm at the store, with Pop and Gram, and even at the diner. Then, when Mr. Hamden passed away, what a community! I think I like it here. I want to stay." She got teary-eyed when she said the words out loud. She realized that she meant every word. "I want to take over the store and live here, permanently." She said the last sentence and started to cry. *Stop crying, Maude,* she thought to herself.

Liam stood up and invited her for a hug. "I could not be prouder of you. I did a great job raising you!" He laughed and kissed the top of her head. "Pop and Gram love you as if you were their own daughter, not only a granddaughter. They were amazing parents and as you can tell by now, they're good business people and pillars in this community," he said.

"I guess that's why you work so hard. You're just like them!" She laughed through her tears.

They hugged again and sat down on the foot of the bed. Just then, Liam's phone beeped. He reached for it. He read an email out loud. "It's from Gabriel. He said he has some answers about the gold coins. Wants to meet later today, if we're able to." Liam read. "Let's break the news to Pop and Gram about Tommy first. I'll see if Ned can come by this morning. I think we can do this with just him. I'll give Gabriel a call a little later."

With that, they hugged and gave cheek kisses and made plans to meet in the kitchen in a half an hour. Ned texted he'd be at the house then, and Maude continued getting ready as her dad excused himself to take a shower. Maude took several deep breaths and sat down to pray. *Lord, this is a ton to take in. I worry about Gram understanding all this. It's sad Tommy isn't here to talk to, for them to get to know each other. I wonder if there are pictures to comfort Gram with.* Suddenly Maude remembered the picture inside her grandma's Bible. She could remind her of that if she got upset. *Thank you, Lord. Give us strength, the wisdom of your words, and peace more than anything. In Jesus' name I pray, Amen.* Maude finished the prayer, and despite the knots in her stomach, she opened the door to her bedroom and made her way to the kitchen with as big a smile as she could muster.

It was all quiet in the kitchen. She vaguely heard the shower going, but otherwise, the ticking clock on the wall and the refrigerator clicking on seemed to echo within the room. As she neared the cupboard and reached her hand to grab a teacup, she felt a prickle on that hand. Instantly, she smiled. "Hi, Mom," she whispered. As always, her mom showed up at the exact moment she needed her to give a wink of comfort. It never crossed Maude's mind to feel weird or scared in these moments. In fact, she specifically remembered when she first saw flickering specks at a very young age. It was her first day of kindergarten. Her excitement was overwhelming and as Gram pinned her hair up that morning, Maude saw a flicker in the corner of the room. At first, she put it out of her mind. But when it happened again a few seconds later, she knew it wasn't *just her eyes playing tricks on her*. Oh, how many times she had heard grownups say things like that. At the time, she was too young to realize the deeper meaning behind it but grew to realize that perhaps those times weren't merely tricks of the eyes for others. But she still didn't mention it to Gram that morning. Gram had been there for a week to enjoy Maude's first week of school, and the rush and excitement to get to school overtook her.

Later that same week, Maude saw the flickers two more times. That was when she knew it was something substantial and not an isolated event. Though not old enough to have solid memories of her mom, she still learned it was okay to talk to her as if she was there because her dad and Pop and Gram said her mom would be with her always as her guardian angel. So,

Maude pretended Hazel was there and on the last morning of that first week, which would be Gram's last school morning before she would head back to Ardendale, Maude cried. It made her sad to think of not having Gram around for the school mornings. But no sooner did Maude think this that she felt a nudge—not a physical one but a stirring within her heart—and saw the flickering off in the distance. This was also the first time she could distinctly smell lilacs. In fact, she'd even asked her Gram if her perfume was lilac-scented because it was that strong—but she had not brought perfume with her!

Back in the kitchen, Maude grabbed a teacup about a fictional holiday village called Gommet—she loved that children's book; it was her favorite. She grabbed a tea bag and hot water from the dispenser, and as she stirred, the flickering started. If it wasn't so common for Maude to see, sense, feel, and hear all these various things, she would have chalked up the circumstances as fruit flies or something teeny tiny or even her eyes playing tricks on her, but as the years passed and it happened—along with other comforts—she knew better.

"Pretty crazy stuff, huh, Mom?" she whispered.

Alas, her mom didn't speak in words or sounds that anyone other than Maude would understand, but Maude felt and *heard* her mom's comfort and reassurance of good things to come.

A tremendous amount of stress lifted off Maude's shoulders when at last, two hours later, the hard talk over breakfast—and the tears—were over. Ned and Liam had articulately explained everything to Pop and Gram. Gram, of course, was more emotional than Pop, but she held it together well considering how life-changing this was. Her tears were sympathetic for the loss of a family she never knew and for not having the opportunity to really get to know Mr. Hamden other than a polite hello through the years. Liam had the biggest look of relief among them all. The light in his eyes returned, and he no longer looked like death warmed over. Maude felt relief her dad was going to be sticking around for a few more days. Sometimes reality doesn't hit for a while, and she didn't want to be alone to handle it all on her own if her grandparents had a hard time with the facts later on.

Ned's wife invited everyone over for a family-style dinner at their house, which was near the diner. Pop and Gram decided to take the entire day off work, and Liam and Maude spent quality time with them, reading the newspaper, watching *The Young and the Restless,* having coffee and orange juice, ordering take out from the diner for lunch, and simply relaxing. It was the precious few hours they all needed. Around two in the afternoon, Liam and Maude went over to the Bible Church to see Gabriel while Pop and Gram took naps. The church parking lot was well-shaded by the woods surrounding it, and the church's dark red bricks and brilliant stained-glass windows were welcoming after such a busy morning. They walked into the sanctuary where Gabriel was finishing talking to Marc.

"Hi, again!" Marc said enthusiastically. "Setting up for Vacation Bible School," he said, pointing around the church. Maude noticed a "Fishers of Men, Matthew 4:19" sign and boxes full of kid things—posters, streamers, buckets, fishing nets, colorful wands, and neat looking uniforms. Maude blushed, feeling the crush she had on Marc revealing itself through the color creeping up her face.

"We'll be over in my home office if you need anything," Gabriel said to Marc and pointed to the rooms behind the sanctuary, hidden by its walls. Maude heard voices as well as tape being ripped and a hammer banging, signifying other church members were setting up their rooms as well. "Follow me, you two," Gabriel said as he looked at Maude and Liam.

"See you later!" Marc said to Maude. He even winked at her. She definitely blushed then, unable to hide it.

Maude was trying to think of something to say to him. All she could come up with was something silly. "This place is looking great! Can't wait to see it when it's done!" she said, pasting a smile on her face, embarrassed.

"We could use help at VBS if you're interested. Lots of kids, not enough adult hands," Marc said, and Maude didn't say anything. "Let me know." He reached into his back pocket and pulled out a business card and handed it to her. Maude smiled back, pleased with the thought of helping at the church.

"Okay! I'll give it some thought," she said, and headed out the side door that led to stone steps and the front door of the parsonage. The three paused as Gabriel unlocked the door to his office. They walked to a room with beige-colored walls, light blue curtains, a ceiling fan, a large brown wooden desk, a swivel chair, and boxes of paperwork. There were a few shadow boxes leaning against the wall. Upon closer inspection, Maude realized they were very old in appearance, and she didn't quite understand just what they were. There were two seats in front of Gabriel's desk and plastic bags with the numerous pipes and gold coins on the center of the desk.

"How's everyone doing?" Gabriel said as some papers blew from the ceiling fan and made a whispering sound. He pointed to the two seats opposite where he sat. Maude and Liam sat down. She looked around the room once more. "You'll have to excuse my clutter. I collect civil war artifacts. Over there against the wall are old muskets and civil war memorabilia. It's been a lifelong hobby of mine." He paused.

He grabbed his coffee cup but put it down quickly. "I'm sorry. Would you like something to drink?" he asked them. Both Maude and Liam shook their heads. "Okay then," Gabriel said and turned to Maude. "Maude, I understand your dad has made you aware of the Mr. Hamden situation. I was able to contact Lester to try to make sense of things." He swallowed, then continued, "If this is too much information right now, we can certainly do this later," he offered.

Liam looked at Maude then back at Gabriel. "We're all handling it better than expected. I think we're just as curious about this as we were with the Tommy situation," Liam said to Gabriel. "This coin mystery may be just the break we need from the crazy news we received yesterday," he commented.

"Well, I'm afraid this may or may not be a break," Gabriel said. He reached over for a handheld magnifier and placed it carefully over one of the pipes securely placed in a see-through bag. "Upon closer inspection, I found a small handwritten letter just on the inside of the pipes. *All the pipes.* It appears to be the letter H. It is what I suppose would be a family crest." He looked at the symbol again.

"No way," Liam said.

"In the same way people may have their checks personalized with the first letter of their last name, these pipes have an H handwritten on them, small and precise. It is obviously not professionally done, but it's clear these are all from the same person or entity. That alone helped me to narrow this down. I knew we weren't working with random people putting gold coins into pipes. As weird as that'd be, as an historian, I have to rule things out." Gabriel put the magnifier to the side and carefully moved the bag to the left. He pulled over a binder and opened it. "The woods that are there now weren't always woods. In the 1800s, people lived there and the town that we know today was mostly woods, including right where we're sitting. Given people moving and things being torn down, the families that lived there 200 plus years ago are not necessarily the ancestors of the families that live in town now."

Liam squinted. "I explained this to Maude, the way the town switched, for the lack of a better term."

Gabriel nodded. "With God's help, I was able to discover that the foundation belonged to George O'Brien. He lived there with his wife, Claire. They had one child, George O' Brien Jr. In 1861, George Sr. went to serve in the Civil War. Prior to that, he worked on the railroads. Railroad jobs back then included building tracks and steam engines and keeping them both in good working order. His wife Claire was a housewife and dressmaker. Due to a back injury, she no longer could work in the fields during harvest time as she had before George Jr. was born. Unfortunately, George Sr. died at war. He received a bounty for signing up, which he gave to his wife, and then in the event of his death, she was given a widow's pension. Further, because George Jr. was young, she received a children's relief amount each month until he was eighteen."

He watched as Maude and Liam glanced at the binder. He gave them a minute to look at the paperwork, which consisted mostly of names.

"Okay, so these were her gold coins within the pipes?" Maude asked Gabriel.

Gabriel nodded. "When George died, Claire survived on the government pension, but she was profoundly frugal. She didn't trust banks, made clothes for herself and her son, and mended others' clothing. Her customers paid with a nickel here, a quarter there. She saved a lot. I'm afraid she didn't appear to have a warmth about her. She was all business and though a good parent, I didn't find much in terms of friends or connections. That's not to say she didn't have friends, but her reputation appears to have been about work and motherhood, nothing in between."

Gabriel opened a second binder. "These gold coins are a combination of years and years of seamstress work, her husband's pension, and the bounty. The children's relief fund was given to her son, but she'd saved so much that she had to do something with it. Since she didn't trust banks to keep her money safe, she exchanged her money for gold coins. The pipes where the gold coins were found appear to be made of similar material to what the railroad tracks are built from. Since her husband built railroads, this would make sense. She put these coins into the pipes, and they were buried." He stopped talking and sat back in his chair.

Liam looked some more at the papers then spoke up. "Okay, so these gold coins belonged to Claire O'Brien? She made and fixed clothes and cashed all monies into gold coins, including any funds she received from her husband's untimely death? Do I have that straight?"

Gabriel nodded.

"So, what happens to these coins now?" Liam asked. "How much are they worth?" he asked as he leaned forward, almost whispering the question.

"Here comes the crazy part," Gabriel responded. "Claire was O'Brien by marriage. But her maiden name? Are you ready for this?" He paused and looked back and forth between Maude and Liam. "Claire Holmes, as in the many generations ago grandmother to Tommy Hamden." Maude and Liam's jaws hit the floor.

Suddenly, Maude jumped out of her seat, remembering something. "There is a picture in Gram's Bible of a woman. She is sewing and there are things in the photo, maybe gold, I don't know."

"Wow, there is a photo and a Bible?!" Gabriel's eyebrows shot up. "What else can you tell me about the photo? Do you know where the Bible and photo are?" Gabriel asked.

"The woman is sitting in a rocking chair, I think. She is sitting next to a dog. Gram said it is a grandma of hers, that she doesn't know much more, but it's a relative and she cherishes it. The Bible, too, was from her grandma, she told me." Maude looked first at her dad then at Gabriel. "So, the woman in the photo? Did she also sew, and this is some crazy coincidence, or?

"It isn't her grandma at all. It could be Claire," Gabriel finished her thought.

"Where is this Bible and photo?" Liam asked Maude.

"It was under the counter at the store. I found it and Gram was actually crying because she thought she'd lost it. It clearly meant a lot to her. She said it was a distant grandmother of hers." Maude shook her head. "This is all very confusing," Maude said, trying to make a joke.

"I'd like to see both. It may shed some light," Gabriel said.

"I think, in light of recent developments, Mom would be fine with us borrowing them," Liam said to Gabriel. "I think we could ask for it regarding the family tree, not in regard to the gold coins. They don't know anything about these coins yet." Liam looked at Gabriel. "But if they were on Tommy's family's side, what happens to the coins now?" Liam asked.

Gabriel responded. "The property the coins were on belongs to the village. But given the means by which the coins were located, complete within labeled pipes and in mint condition, in theory they'd belong to Tommy's estate. I almost wish I didn't know about this. I'm afraid many people would have taken this money and run." He looked over at the gold coins. "Legally, it's not as easy as *finders, keepers*, as I was explaining on the hike. If no one knew about this, you could technically take these and no one would know the better. But the fact of the matter is, we have to do the right thing. I couldn't live with myself if we didn't." Gabriel shook his head and looked off into the distance. "I'm preaching here. I don't mean to," Gabriel said.

"No, no, you're right, Gabriel. We are going to do the right thing," Liam responded.

"I agree." Maude smiled, and she truly meant it.

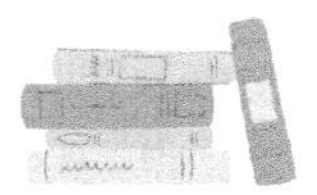

Liam and Maude headed home to see Gram for a short time. They asked her to borrow the picture and Bible regarding the recent developments with Mr. Hamden's will. The photo could possibly shed some light on family. Gram agreed, of course. The suspicion, curiosity, and mystery plagued Maude, and she knew by her Gram's far-away look, that she, too, felt perplexed. They headed back to the church to show Gabriel. Maude held the box on her lap, feeling like the Bible and photo were fragile and the key to unlocking a crazy puzzle.

In Gabriel's office a mere forty-five minutes later, Gabriel carefully opened the contents of the box. When he pulled the photo out, Liam looked it over, and Maude sat in silence.

Suddenly, she remembered something else. "Oh my gosh, I forgot about this. When I visited Mr. Hamden's store and he gave me the rocking chair, which I know you've been made aware of, Mr. Titus, he also showed me all this drapery material." She pointed to the material in the photo. "He said that it was in the store when he inherited it and that it was drapery material, which was cheaper to make clothing from. Actually, I recognized the pattern in the store from seeing it in this photo originally. He gave me the material, and it's been sitting in a box in the trunk of my car." She looked from her dad to Gabriel.

There was a long silence as Gabriel studied the photo. Liam looked over the page the Bible was opened to, afraid to touch it. Gabriel slid the photo over to Liam with a cloth and used gloves to leaf delicately through the Bible. Maude sat in silence, trying to take everything in.

"Wow," Gabriel said. "This is Claire in the photo, but Marguerite thinks it's Christine. It is possible Christine also sewed, but these things in the photo—it's too coincidental. When I look closely at the table, it appears there are pipes sitting on it. I know it's difficult to make out. Could Christine also have collected coins? I guess she could, maybe. But my instinct is that this is Claire. But how did the Bible end up in Marguerite's possession? If a grandma had given it to her, is it possible they knew about the twins? I don't know if we'll ever know," Gabriel's voice trailed off. "On the inside cover of the Bible is that same handwritten letter H. It must have been Claire's. I can look through it to see if we can come up with any more clues." Both Liam and Maude looked at each other and nodded.

"Whatever you can do. Maude and I can go and come back or if you need to look later," Liam said.

"No, I have time now," Gabriel responded. Just then his cell phone rang. "Excuse me for just a second." Maude stifled a giggle when she saw his old-fashioned flip cellular phone that was not touch screen.

"Hi, Marc. Bernie? Oh, yes, okay, I will be right there." He hit the end button on his old-fashioned cell. "I just have to help Bernie and Shirley with a quick something. Are you guys alright here for a moment?" he asked.

"Of course. In the meantime, can we be of any assistance right now with anything else?" Liam asked.

"Actually, to be honest, we could use some help setting up in the church. I know you meant here with the mystery before us, but I would like to take time to go through this, and if you have time, we could really use the help over there," Gabriel added.

"Of course, we can help." Liam looked at Maude. She nodded. "We'll go over there and do what we can and will check in with you a little later," Liam replied.

"Excellent. I'll walk over with you right now so I can help Bernie. Then, I'll come back and see if I find anything," Gabriel said.

Chapter Nine

While Liam headed off to help some of the older church members to set up for VBS, Marc asked Maude to help him. "I'm doing the junior high program for VBS this year," Marc told her.

"I remember you saying that at the diner. You usually do the youth group for church; did I remember that right?" she asked him, somehow feeling less shy and nervous.

"Yep! The youth group has really grown. I love it. How awkward was I at that age, and to help thirteen-year-olds feel less awkward? I am happy to do it," Marc enthusiastically replied.

Somehow Maude couldn't picture Marc as awkward. He was handsome, extroverted, and helpful. She remembered him saying he was part of the fire department, too, and she'd met him because of the EMT situation. He worked for the church too? Suddenly, she felt inept. She knew she shouldn't think it, but the thought crossed her mind—what a catch he must be. As if he read her thoughts, he spoke up. "I have a lot going on. But I could use help with the youth group. You were going to stick around, right?" he asked her.

"Yes," she said with certainty. "I'm going to be taking over the store. At least attempting to, *someday*." She laughed at herself. "My dad can't leave what I used to call home due to his job, and my grandparents have no one else. I wasn't sure what I wanted to do, but I've come to actually want to stick around," she replied, once again surprised at the truth in her words. She kept half expecting to chicken out, but she continued to want to stay put.

"That is awesome! If you ever want to come here, I'd love the help," Marc said, then winked at her.

She felt the butterflies in her stomach again. "I'd love to help. Even when we didn't get to church, I believe and practice my Christian faith, so I would love to get involved," she commented. "But I think, selfishly, it'll help me when my dad goes back home. I'm going to miss him." She surprised herself at how open she was being with Marc.

"I get it. Well, please, come here, meet new people, get involved. You can help me. You'll fit right in," he said and paused. "Heck, you already do! Here you are setting up with me!" Marc grinned.

"True!" she replied. There was a pause while they hung a banner. "I'll plan to come, what the heck? Your grandpa has been wonderful to me and my family." She picked up a poster from a box. "What do you want me to do with these?" Before he could answer, Liam and Gabriel came through the side door with a couple about the same age as Liam.

"Hey, Maude, I want you to meet my parents!" Marc said to Maude enthusiastically. Maude stood up. A woman came over who was plump, about Maude's height with straight, shoulder-length brown hair and defined dimples. Maude extended her hand. "This is my mom, Adelaide." Maude and Adelaide smiled at each other. "And this is my dad, Earl," Marc said as Maude shook hands with a tall, chunky man with short, combed-over gray hair.

"Hello, Maude!" Adelaide said to her. She was bubbly and instantly gave Maude a warm feeling. "We haven't seen your dad in years and are so glad to finally see you again! I don't think we've seen you since you were a small little girl." She put her hand at her waist to signify a child who was young and short. "Your dad tells me you are sticking around! How wonderful. If we can help you in the transition, let us know!" she offered, making Maude want to hug her. Earl smiled along with Adelaide.

"It is so nice to meet you!" Maude replied, smiling at Adelaide, telepathically sending thoughts of warmth, gratitude, and even love to this woman who seemed to brighten the room. That was when Maude felt that brush, that tickle, that *feeling* on her shoulder. She smiled and thought, *Thank you, Mom.*

"Okay, I need to head back to my office. Let me know if you need anything," Gabriel said to Adelaide and Earl. "Marc, can you check on Bernie and Shirley in the foyer once in a while? Everything is already hung up, but make sure they don't lift tables or anything, sheesh," he said to Marc.

"Pops!" Marc said, shaking his head and smiling to himself. Maude remembered him referring to Bernie as Pops at the diner.

Gabriel went back to his office. Liam and Adelaide and Earl went over to the far end of the sanctuary. They sorted through some papers.

"Bernie and Shirley's twin sons are both out of state with their families. The whole town thinks of Bernie and Shirley as their adopted grandparents, and I guess I'm no exception." He smiled. "That's why it meant so much when you helped them at your store," he said, picking up the stapler and walking over to the large bulletin board.

"I just called the ambulance. But they seem to be lovable old people," Maude said. She decided there was no sense in fighting the *hero* label she'd been given for such a simple act. She knew it was a big deal to everyone else. Now that she knew what neat people they were, she understood how much even the simplest act of kindness would mean to a town of people who adored them.

"So, VBS starts this coming week? I don't see why I can't come help out." Maude was again surprised at her boldness.

"Great! Last I knew, Grandpa needed someone to check kids in, and I could certainly use the help in my group," Marc said. He stapled up a poster.

Maude read the first few lines, noticing each letter had a Biblical connotation. A: Ambitious (Matthew 5:6), D: Devoted (Colossians 3:17), V: Verse Learning (Proverbs 18:15).

He continued, interrupting her thoughts. "I mean it. I'd love the help. I need help just keeping things in order, mostly." There was a pause. "So, what do you like to do in your spare time?" he asked her.

"I like to write and read," Maude said, looking up and trying to think about what else she did with her free time. "I never pictured myself running a store. Honestly, I felt I was too reserved for that. But the people have been receptive, and I look forward to it. Truthfully, I hadn't found my niche back home. I think I have here." She smiled, happy that she was feeling so open with Marc.

Booming laughter erupted from the other side of the wall. Bernie and Shirley's laughter echoed from the small room they were in. Marc and Maude both laughed at the sound. It was impossible not to. Adelaide, Earl, and Liam all looked in that direction and laughed too.

In that precise moment, Maude was feeling wonderful about her future in Ardendale. It wasn't necessarily the laughter, the almost-solved coin mystery, the new family tree, Marc, or even having her dad staying a few extra days that gave her peace. It was her faith. She felt the Lord working things out just as He promised he would long ago in Romans 8:28. "And we know that in all things God works for the good of those who love him, who have been called according to his purpose."

Things at the store were all going in a positive direction, and she felt confident in her ability to someday take over. She felt relief knowing she had years to get things right and was grateful for the current manager's willingness to help. Now she also looked forward to getting involved with the church. She remembered her dad telling stories of attending this very church and how he loved it. Heck, she was even warming up to Marc after having been terrible shy and nervous around him. She was meeting wonderful people and things felt great. And her mom was with her. She knew it, felt it, and cherished it.

The question of the ownership of the gold coins was the only question left in her mind. She pondered what would happen in the town when word got out about the findings. All she could do was to wait and pray. Once in a while, she and her dad eyed each other and smiled. He was helping with things, too, and she ached for him to stick around forever. She supposed that was the only sad situation within the picture she had of the bright future.

It was several hours before they heard from Gabriel. He'd called Liam to tell him he was going to see Marian McCarthy. Liam and Maude left church and spent a wonderful rest of the day with Philly and Marguerite and dinner with Ned and Lucy. On occasion, Maude saw Liam gazing off into the distance with a look of sadness in his eyes. Somehow Maude just knew her dad was feeling sad about leaving his family in Ardendale in a few days. They didn't talk about the gold coins. Pop and Gram and Maude and Liam did talk about Mr. Hamden's possessions and that

Gram would donate them. She said Gabriel had connections through church families and organizations in need, so she'd give whatever was left to them. They spoke of Tommy once in a while that evening, the occasional interactions they had with him, and they spoke of his parents, who they'd known only briefly.

Maude found herself wondering if she'd handle things as well as Gram had if she were in her shoes. Eventually, she asked Gram, "You're handling all this extremely well. To find out there were identical twins and a long line of family on both sides, and that you had family right here in Ardendale. That is wild!" Maude said to her.

Gram nodded. "It is crazy. What am I going to do, though? If knowing he had some family was some sort of solace to Tommy before he passed, then to God be the glory," Gram said. "His business was successful, and he was a good man, and it sounds like I had a wonderful heritage. Life is life. I only wish we'd gotten to know him more closely. That's a shame." She wiped imaginary dust off from the table.

Gram was a pillar of strength in Maude's eyes. She carried herself with integrity and professionalism. She was beautiful—she and Pop both were—still carrying on a business that hadn't slowed down despite their increasing, though still healthy, ages. Maude realized she hadn't had much of a womanly presence to look up to and now she had one in her Gram. She could learn from her and the way The Books Are Here was still booming. It spoke volumes for what wonderful business people her grandparents were. She remembered one year nearly ten years ago when Pop and Gram were honored by the local Chamber of Commerce for being the "Business People of the Year," and she and her dad had come to town to celebrate during one short weekend in March. The weather had been terrible; they'd only been able to stay in town for a few hours beyond the dinner, and she was young so she didn't remember the entire evening, but she did remember thinking at the time that Pop and Gram must be pretty awesome people. Now, she knew it to be absolute truth.

As the night wore on and everyone grew tired, they said goodnight, and all headed to bed. Maude thought how Pop and Gram still didn't know anything about the coins, but for now, it was best to find out more information before they approached her about the big news. Tommy's family connection was enough for now.

Across town, Gabriel and Marian were sifting through the facts. Marian came to a responsible conclusion that she thought would please everyone.

The next morning, Gabriel, Liam, Ned, and Maude met, this time at his office near the Emporium. Marian was there, too, and they sat in circle around a table that had the gold coins, pipes, Bible, photo, the family tree, and will out.

Marian said a lot of legal mumbo jumbo to them, and finally, in layman's terms started, "The coins were buried. Clearly, they were meant to be handed down to future generations in Claire's family. It is our best guess that the dog in the photo buried the pipes. Who knows why? But, is it coincidence that Copper found the coins? We know that many families in town had one or two families of Dobermans through the years. Could it be that Copper somehow smelled his dog relatives? It's all wild but food for thought." Marian paused, looking at everyone in turn.

"But back to the situation at hand. When the house was demolished and trees and woods replaced that area of town, the ownership of the goods was lost. The village owns the land where the pipes were found, and therefore, we cannot in good conscious give everything over to you. However, we've come up with something that we think is fair. Liam, as a lawyer, we know that this conversation must stay only within these walls." Marian looked at Maude.

"Yes, ma'am," Maude replied, inching closer to her dad.

"Of course. What is the plan?" Liam asked.

"These coins are worth thousands, William," Marian continued. "I can't even comprehend how rare these are. The total monetary value is too abundant to even discuss, in fact. We'd like to make a compromise with you. While the coins are in your family line, the land belongs to the village. We'd like to use the gold coins to revitalize this town. It could give the failing businesses a chance to turn around. And in turn, we can brainstorm how to bring more people to Ardendale. This is a beautiful, scenic area but unfortunately, it's turned into a bedroom community in that people live here but work elsewhere. Let's use this money to turn things around. Let's make this town what it was 100 years ago!" Marian almost shouted.

No one responded, expecting her to say more, and eventually, she did. "However, we cannot ignore the fact that the property where the coins were found belonged to your family. It was Marguerite and Tommy's family. Again, the land legally belongs to the village now and has for over 100 years. But we cannot deny that the coins were most likely meant to be given to the family line to come. It is a fine line we walk here. The fact of the matter is, Maude and Ned, and you guys, too, were all honest about this. You could have walked away with your findings and never told anyone. No one would have known any differently. So, taking all those factors into consideration, we want to reward Maude and Ned both for their honesty in this. A third of the total amount will be split between the two of you, contingent upon complete discretion of the exact amount on your parts." Marian sat back in her chair.

"Okay," Maude and Ned said in unison. Maude was numb

with all the details, but it sounded fair. She knew her dad would not agree to anything that wasn't on the up and up. *Man, thank God my dad is a lawyer,* she thought.

"In the same way some celebrities get married and their guests must sign *silence clauses,* this will be something similar. Whether you use the amount toward retirement or a vacation or education, we have no say in that. You just would need to be quiet about the amount you received," Marian said, pulling a binder out of the messenger bag next to her chair.

"Of course, she will," Liam said to Marian regarding Maude. "Ned would do the same."

"The money we give is going to be recorded, but frankly, the townspeople don't need to know the exact dollar amount that was found. It could cause commotion and frankly, it's no one's business," Marian said. Liam reached into his front pocket and pulled out his glasses. He put them on and read over the paper. Maude fidgeted in her seat. Ned sat silently.

"This paperwork just says that money was found on village property and is being donated to the village. Because the finders were honest and open with their findings, they are being rewarded for their honesty," Liam read aloud to Maude.

"Okay, so Ned and Maude, to be clear, the town will use the gold coins to revitalize itself, but there won't be any discussion of the where or what precisely happened," Liam explained to Ned and Maude in the same way he explained legal mumbo jumbo to his clients.

"Correct," Marian responded.

"Thank you. I appreciate this," Maude replied. Ned nodded. Ned was clearly calm, as he always was. It was no surprise to her that he remained this way despite the circumstances.

"Let's talk a little about this," Liam said to Ned and Maude. They excused themselves onto the other side of the room. "This is completely fair," he said. "I think you guys should agree to this. The amount of money you'll each receive . . . Let's say you'll be secure for the rest of your lives," Liam said to them.

"Good thing we have a lawyer on hand!" Ned laughed. *My thoughts exactly,* Maude thought. "This is wonderful. I say okay. I mean this is more than fair." He looked at Maude, who nodded.

"Dad, you know best," Maude said.

"Okay, so it's a go?" Liam asked. Both Ned and Maude said yes and walked back over to Marian.

"I took the liberty of drawing up papers. There is no hurry on signing these. Please take your time to think things through," Marian offered.

"Thanks, Marian. But we're ready now," Liam responded.

"Ah, the privilege of having a lawyer for a client!" Marian joked. "Seriously, I will keep you in the loop on everything I find out, Liam," she said, sliding papers across the desk to the crew.

They sat and reviewed each page. Liam gave simple terms on what each page meant, and Ned and Maude signed when instructed. Marian occasionally interjected something, and Liam smiled with each signature in his reassuring way.

"Now to tell Mom and Dad," Liam said.

As they trickled out of the room at the end of the meeting, Maude felt a sense of relief about the coins. She hadn't realized before today that she had felt some apprehension about what would happen with them. Immediately, she thought she'd like to pay off Pop and Gram's debts, invest in the future of the store, and help her dad out. But she'd have that conversation later when things cooled down and more details ironed out. In the meantime, she and Liam said they'd make a plan and knew Ned would make a wise decision with his share of the money as well.

Liam's phone chimed as they neared the rental car. He lifted it from his back pocket and glanced at it. "Wow. Seven missed calls from Dad! But it hasn't rung until now. What?!" He called his voicemail and his eyes got big as saucers. "Oh, no. Maudie,

Gram's taken ill. She's on her way to the hospital." Liam lost all the color in his face. He fumbled for his keys, physically having an adverse reaction to the news. "They think she had a stroke," he said, barely able to speak.

Maude didn't know what to say. She immediately started to cry, feeling nauseated. "We're going to get there to help her, Dad." She mustered out an encouraging phrase but felt torn up on the inside. "Did Pop say anything else?" she asked.

"He found her on the ground. She was breathing, but . . ." his voice trailed off. He swallowed. She heard his gulp. "She was confused and couldn't walk," he replied. His phone rang again. "Dad, we're on our way!" he said into the phone. "What! Dad? No! What?! Mom is? Wait until I get there; don't let anyone do anything else. Tell Mom we're on our way." Maude heard her dad yell as she stared in his direction. It was clear something else had happened and when she glanced forward to gather her thoughts, she saw an oncoming car.

"Dad! Watch out!" She reached for the steering wheel to yank their car out of the way.

Visit Felicity's website anytime for her bio, upcoming books,
events, visits,
and for her social media fun!

Made in United States
North Haven, CT
13 April 2022

18196526R00065